VANISHING POINT

Books by Richard S. Platz

Novels

OF MAGIC AND DELUSION

PROJECT DIVINE WIND

APPOINTMENT AT ANGAHUAN
(Co-Authored with James A. Kline)

Short Stories

MEMORIES & OTHER FICTIONS

DREAMTIME

VANISHING POINT

VANISHING POINT

And Other Stories

Blue Lake Press

BLUE LAKE PRESS
A Western Division Subsidiary of the
Chicago, Whitewater & Mad River Company
P O Box 797, Blue Lake, CA 95525

ISBN: 978-0692682845

Contents

Preface

This book is a steam train westward bound. Our old-time carriage trundles from side to side above the clickety-clack of steel wheels on iron rails. We ride in a vintage coach with the redolence of wood smoke from the potbelly in back laced with heavier whiffs of coal smoke from the engine up front. Look, the passengers are from our stories.

Up front on the left a prospector and a woodsman share a crowded bench. Their rucksacks rattle in the luggage rack above them. The prospector is a burly man, but he looks unwell. The woodsman, slender and pale with thin blond hair and a balding pate, appears a little lost.

Across the aisle rides Mrs. Wigmore, a dowdy school marm with a graying bun of wavy brown hair pinned severely against the back of her head. She is smiling at some treasured memory with the children.

Behind the prospector sits Jacob Ramirez, a stout young Papago Indian. His unkempt black hair spills down his forehead and over his ears. A tattered straw Mexican sombrero fidgets nervously on his knee. He is on his way home.

Behind our school marm Evan Layton has closed his eyes. He dreams of returning to the West Coast in first class aboard a vessel of an entirely different sort. And he is not pleased to be going back.

A little ahead of us on the left side, a railroad lawyer and a stagecoach driver are in deep conversation. The lawyer is a lithe, rangy fellow in a charcoal three-piece suit. His companion's face is round and chubby, but tanned and deeply creased from age and too many years in too much sun. His short legs do not quite reach the floor.

Across the aisle, in front of us, are seated Lord and Lady Bingham, but they are not speaking at present. Something has come up concerning the butler that they have been unable to resolve.

And there are other characters, most of them riding in the carriages following behind, for their times have not yet come. But don't worry. You will meet them all as you read these stories. The point is, each of their stories is different. Some are of different times, others of different places, and still others of different realities. But the characters all seem comfortable riding along together in this single volume, and I trust that the reader will share their comfort.

These stories are sung by the rails as we ride. One rail sings of creatures of this ordinary world. River rafters. Backpackers. Stagecoach drivers. None of them famous. Characters who struggle with individual choices in a world no one understands. Characters who evaporate with time. Just like you and me.

The other rail counterpoints with matters a bit more fantastic. Of things we will probably never see. Of the extraordinary. Of the imaginary. Of the quantum mechanical, which is impossible to place entirely in one world or the other.

Yet the two rails do seem to come together in the distance, as far away as the eye can see, just this side of that rusty orange sunset on the horizon. At the vanishing point.

RSP
April 2016
Blue Lake, California

Man Eaten

1

It hit him as he was straining up the steep, rocky approach to the lake. He could feel it jump in his chest, like an automatic transmission shifting gears. The steady pounding became a fluttering. He knew what it was right away. His heart had gone into atrial fibrillation.

"*Oh sweet Jesus!*" he muttered. "Not *now!*"

Ernie Ackerman struggled out of his backpack and let it drop in the dust beside the trail. He eased down and leaned against a granite boulder. This had happened once before, triggered by an intense workout on a StairMaster. "Supraventricular tachycardia" the cardiologist had called it. "Not life threatening, under normal circumstances."

Ernie looked down at his pack. Sixty pounds of dead weight. The rocky trail up the canyon defile was steep and challenging and he was dripping with sweat. The sun was already dropping behind the western cliff. A cool breeze wafted down from the snow fields above. And he was hiking alone.

Not exactly what you might call normal circumstances.

His fingers rubbed the flesh above his breastbone, and Ernie felt fear. *Fragile*, he thought. *Oh, so fragile.* He drained off the rest of his water bottle and tried to get a grip on himself. Leaned back and breathed in the sweet fragrance of pennyroyal and pine. Felt the rock rough against his back, still warm from the sun. Drew in a few deep breaths and listened to his heart trip-hammering and tried to will it to slow down. It did not seem inclined to do so. He felt lightheaded. Tiny black spots floated across his vision. He needed to calm down.

So he took the time to look around. It was some of the most rugged country he had ever hiked through. Stunningly beautiful. The Russian Wilderness. House-sized blocks of granite split off from the cliffs above. Spires of splintered rock at the crest. It was amazing they had been able to blaze a trail through here at all. But they had. The Pacific Crest Trail had been etched and blasted and chipped into the vertical western bedrock wall below Russian Peak and into the precipitous eastern face south of Paynes Lake. Further north, in the Marble Mountain Wilderness, Man Eaten Lake straddled the jagged crest at the head of Wooley Creek. His ultimate destination.

A chill shivered though him, so he crawled over and switched his soaked shirt for a dry one. The SVT was not about to quit. Last time, as he remembered, it had taken hours. Then, when it was finally over, it was over. There were no aftereffects.

But right now he didn't know how to fix it. And he couldn't camp here on the trail and wait it out. There was no water. Nowhere flat to sleep. And he didn't dare haul that sixty-pound pack any further. He had to do something *now*. Ernie drew a deep breath. His only choice was to make multiple trips up to the lake. As many as needed. Haul up what he could each time. He searched through his pack and pulled out the water filter and the tent and the food bag, which was heavily stocked for a ten-day trip. The food bag had its own shoulder straps, so he harnessed it on. He curled the tent under his left arm, gripped the water filter in his left hand and his walking stick in his right, planted one foot firmly in front of the other, and began stumping his way slowly up the trail through a sea of low Sadler Oak. The lake couldn't be much farther.

At the top of a ridge a trail junction sign pointed left to the Pacific Crest Trail and right to the lake. He shifted his burdens from one arm to the other and took the right fork. The path ascended the bank above a ravine choked with alders and willows and ferns before joining the creek for the last hundred yards of the climb.

A terminal moraine held back the big alpine lake and bounded its north shore. The outlet creek had excavated a high notch in the moraine. On a flat above the creek stood a blue tent in a grove of hemlock and red fir, tall and slender and open with massive yellow cones at the crowns. Tiny azaleas ringed the lake's edge, not yet fully bloomed. Directly across the water to the south rose the towering white cirque of granite and talus left by a departing glacier. Patches of snow lingered in the shaded hollows.

A young woman sat on a fallen log by the shore gazing out across the water. The small red hound beside her barked once and trotted over to sniff Ernie. The woman turned and waved. "Don't mind him," she called. "He won't bite."

Slowly he crested the ridge and approached her. "Looks like you . . . got the best . . . campsite."

She was perhaps half his age. Early twenties. Dark gray shorts. Long, tanned legs. Wool socks in hiking boots. An orange down vest hung open and made her torso look short and full. Like a lollipop. She wore her reddish-brown, wavy hair in a ponytail that poked through the back of her green Oregon Ducks cap. Her mouth was wide, her lips full. She was almost pretty, but not quite, until she smiled. Then it all lit up with an inner beauty. "We like it just fine. Plan to stay here another night in fact."

At the edge of her campsite Ernie dropped his tent and food bag and stood panting. Before her stood a tall, bedraggled man in his mid-forties with wild, disheveled brown hair, a hint of gray at the temples, and a whisker-studded chin. He was sturdy, more like a boxer than a long distance runner. His nose looked like it had once been broken and never reset properly, but his face was not unattractive for all that. He might have appeared dangerous, but for the worry in his tired brown eyes.

The dog began sniffing his beached gear.

"What's his . . . name?" Ernie panted.

"Hero."

"Hero," he repeated. He was sweating and couldn't seem to catch his breath. The sound of pounding surf roared in his ears. "Mind if I . . . sit down . . . for a minute?"

"Please do. You're here for the night?"

"If there's . . . any more . . . campsites."

"There's a nice little one up the hill." She pointed up the moraine. "It's small. And a bit exposed. But it's got a fire ring and some rock furniture and an easy trail down to the water."

His heart was still fluttering madly. He rested his elbows on his knees and allowed his head to droop into his hands. Through them he asked, "Room for a tent?"

"Are you alright? You look pale."

"Well . . . that's the thing." He raised his head. "I'm having this

. . . this medical deal here. D'you know what . . . atrial fibrillation . . . is?"

"Yes, I do." Without hesitation she stepped over and placed a cool hand on his forehead. Then she picked up his wrist and encircled it with her slender fingers.

"SVT?" he asked.

"Yes. Shush." She was clocking his pulse with her wrist watch. "A hundred and fifty," she said, concerned.

"Seems about right. You a nurse?"

"Training to become one. I'm taking classes at the college," she said. "Any dizziness?"

"Maybe a little . . . lightheaded."

"Any pain in the chest?"

"Not really."

"Shortness of breath?"

"I just climbed up . . . a couple hundred feet . . . a little winded . . . sure."

"There's no cell phone service here," she said, fumbling for the next issue on a checklist she wished she had learned better.

He shrugged. He hadn't brought a cell phone anyway.

"I better call Bounce." She headed toward the shore and called out across the water, "*Hey Bounce!*"

"Bounce?" Ernie asked.

"My fiancé. He's out fishing off the logs. *Bounce!*" she called again.

"*Yo!*" came a response from somewhere beyond the azaleas.

"*I need you back here! Hurry!*"

"I didn't mean to cause a fuss," Ernie protested.

"No fuss at all." She held out her hand. "My name's Carla."

"Ernie," he replied. His name sounded strange and distant. Like some useless thing he'd left on a shelf back in the flatlands. Something out of place in the wilderness. He shook her hand. "'Bounce' is an unusual name."

"It's his nickname. He plays a lot of basketball."

"Ah. Bounce." He nodded. "Better than 'Dribble,' I guess."

She laughed, and Ernie laughed with her. He couldn't help it. The laughter seemed to shred his cocoon of dread for a moment. It was almost like falling in love.

"Do you think maybe you should lie down?" she asked.

"Naw," he said, and with an effort grunted to his feet. Waited for the lightheadedness to pass. "I've got to get my tent set up . . . before dark."

"There's a clearing on the other side of our tent. It's small, but you're welcome to use it."

Just then a copper-skinned young man in a brown T-shirt and khaki chinos thrashed his way through the azaleas, a fishing pole balanced across his shoulder. He was muscular and wore his curly black hair neatly-cropped. Most likely Latino blood in those veins, Ernie figured. Clean shaven and fit. Maybe six feet tall, which was short for a basket-ball player. Probably a guard. A ball-handler. Bounce.

Hero bounded over to slobber over him. "What's up?" Bounce asked. Then he saw Ernie. "Howdy." He glanced quizzically at his wife-to-be. "What's going on?"

Carla brought the men together and explained the situation. The heart issue. "I offered to let him set up his tent over there."

Ernie saw a flicker of protest in Bounce's eyes and quickly declined. "Thanks for the offer. You folks are very generous. But I think I'll set up at the campsite on up the ridge you were telling me about. Let you have your space." Ernie picked up the food bag and slung it over one shoulder. Bent down for the tent. When he straightened up dizziness spun over him and he wobbled, but stood his ground. It passed. "I've got to get moving and fetch the rest of my stuff before it gets dark."

"Where's the rest of your stuff?" Carla asked.

"Oh, my backpack's down the trail a ways." Ernie nodded in that direction as he turned to climb the hill. "I figure I'll make two trips."

"Bounce'll go get it for you," she offered. "Won't you, honey?"

"No," Ernie objected. "I couldn't let you do that. I'll be okay–"

"Nonsense!" She came alongside and wrestled the food bag off his shoulder. "I'll carry this and show you where the campsite is. It's easy to miss in the rocks." She turned back. "Bounce?"

But Bounce had already leaned his fly rod against a lodgepole pine. "How far down is it?"

Ernie sighed. "About . . . maybe . . . a quarter mile."

"Can you see it from the trail?"

"It's right on the trail. I can't tell you how much I appreciate–"

"Not another word!" Carla insisted, leading the way up the slope with Hero at her heels. "Save your breath for the climb."

They arrived at the campsite just before sunset. A small open space had been cleared of rocks between a massive red fir and a substantial fire ring built up against a blackened granite slab on the downhill side. The slab offered privacy from the campsite below. The clearing looked flat and big enough for his tent. Two tall white firs would make good hammock anchors. A narrow trail zig-zagged down through white pines and brush to a stand of skeletal lodgepole pines in the wetter region beside the lake. Carla wanted to help him set up the tent, but Ernie refused. So she commandeered his water filter and an empty bottle and descended the little trail to the lake to pump water for him. When she returned, he drank half a liter in one gulp and insisted that he was feeling better and could manage everything else by himself.

"Alright then. But you call us if you need anything. And we'll check up on you later this evening."

"Tomorrow morning will be soon enough." He thanked her and watched those lean firm legs and bouncing ponytail descend the rocky moraine for the last time.

He had erected his tent and was stringing up the hammock when Bounce arrived with the backpack. It was already growing dark. They exchanged pleasantries and talked a little basketball, but Bounce did not tarry long.

Ernie dug out his headlamp and started a small fire to heat water for a freeze-dried dinner. While it heated, he skidded down the steep trail to fetch more water in a plastic gallon milk jug, then trudged slowly back up to camp to pump it into his bottle. His heart was still fibrillating, but at least the heavy climbing was over for the day. He switched into a dry pile pullover and an old pair of battered running shoes, then ate slouched in the hammock, swaying gently, as frogs began to croak and darkness engulfed the lake. He felt much better as his belly filled with hot Turkey Tetrazzini. It had been a hell of an afternoon.

After dinner Ernie inflated his air mattress, unstuffed his sleeping bag, and inserted them into the tent. As was his habit, he hung his backpack from a nail he found about six feet up the gnarly, lichen-covered trunk of the big red fir. He folded the rest of his gear inside the pack with his hiking boots on top so critters couldn't gnaw the sweaty laces for the salt. Then he went to find a branch from which to hang his food out of reach of the bears. There weren't a lot of big trees on the moraine, but in the narrow beam of his headlamp he found a small one that would do, tossed a line over a low branch, and pulled the food bag up and tied it off.

Tired, but reasonably content, Ernie lay in the hammock and watched the stars come out. He thought about Carla and Bounce. He would have been in a world of hurt if they hadn't been there to help him. Paying it forward was what they were doing. What goes around comes around. He had been lucky. Nice folks. Pretty girl. Long legs. And studying to be a nurse.

As he was gazing at the Milky Way, watching it materialize, his heart suddenly jumped back into its normal rhythm. Just like that. He could feel it happen. Just like the last time. And Ernie started to feel whole again. The worst was over. All he had to do was take it a bit easier the next few days, and everything was going to be as right as rain. Tomorrow would be a day of rest.

2

He woke abruptly in the night. Something bad was about to happen. Ernie could feel it. Something *else* bad. Not his heart. This had nothing to do with the palpitations and fluttering. His heart was thudding along with a fine, steady beat. No, this would be something else.

He rolled onto his stomach and drew the sleeping bag up over his shoulders against the cool night air. His elbows pressed through the thin pad to the gravel beneath the tent floor. The moon had set. Through the mosquito netting he could just make out the paleness of impending dawn in the valley notch to his left. To the east. Above him the starlit granite bulk of the canyon headwall loomed a pale white. A sparkle of bright stars shimmered in the dark water of the basin below.

He listened to the night. It was eerily quiet. The crickets had fallen silent. The frogs down by the water had stopped croaking. The world was holding its breath.

He heard it coming. Before he felt anything, he heard it coming. From the distant meadows below came a low-frequency groan, a sort of weary rumbling of the earth, which grew and echoed and merged with the cliffs above. An oncoming freight train, slow but irresistible. He had enough time to wonder what the hell was going on.

Then the shaking started. Gentle at first, a rocking, then a swaying that left him disoriented and a little woozy, like a landlubber on a gently pitching deck. The first jolt struck with a gut punch that almost knocked him over. He heard his pots and bowl tumble off their stone perch beside the fire pit. Heard the tinkling and clattering of talus falling down the mountain slope in the darkness. Rocks splashed into the lake. Something big rolled, vibrating the earth. A boulder probably.

The ground was lurching badly, rising and falling in broken-elevator jerks and fits like a drunken boxer. A tree branch cracked and thudded into the ground nearby. A big one. Instinctively Ernie curled into a fetal ball with his arms and sleeping bag covering his head, listening for the tree that would crush the tent or the tumbling bolder that would squash him flat.

When the shaking began to subside, he raised his head and straightened out and tried to get it all together in his mind. Then another big wave rolled in from the west, stronger than ever. On and on it went, for what seemed like an eternity. He swayed and bounced, airborne at times, waiting for it to end. He couldn't have crawled out of the tent if he'd wanted to.

Somewhere above him the mountain groaned. A terrible crackling rent the air. He heard tons of bedrock split away from the cliff face and collapse and slide and tumble into the lake with a roaring tidal concussion. He curled his fingers and toes into the tent floor and waited for the displacement wave to surge across the dark water, hoping his camp was perched high enough on the moraine to keep from being scoured over the lip and into the canyon below.

The crest of a lateral wave punched in through the mouth of his tent, ripping out the guy ropes and collapsing the superstructure on top of him. The cold water washed over his sleeping bag, but cradled in the wet nylon of the tent and the soaked down of his bag, his position held. The ground stakes held.

Jesus! he thought helplessly. *Carla and Bounce! My God!*

They would be gone now. He knew that. No way they could have survived the full brunt of that churning tsunami down by the outlet. They had taken that fine campsite and had forced Ernie upward into this smaller, rockier spot. That had saved his life. He was lucky.

Carla and Bounce and Hero were not so lucky.

Guilt pounded through his adrenalized veins. He buried himself in the wet debris. Shivering. Waiting for the ground to stop sloshing. That's what it felt like. Sloshing. The solid earth felt more like a liquid than a solid. Or perhaps a colloid. It did not grow quiet for a long time. He counted his breaths. His heartbeats. And waited.

3

Ernie did not crawl out of that wet nest until he could barely feel any more ground movement. His hands and feet had grown cold and numb. He peeled off the sodden sleeping bag and fumbled with the zipper of the tent door, throwing it back and extracting himself slowly from the wet wreckage. Perhaps it was only in his mind now, all that swaying, but he felt like a sailor taking his first unsteady steps on dry land.

Dust hung low and heavy in the air. The peak of the headwall blazed a lurid red in the first rays of sunlight. Barefoot, Ernie climbed the granite slab which anchored the drowned fire pit. The landscape had been rearranged. A new island of collapsed rock rose above the waters of the far half of the lake. No, not an island. A peninsula, still connected to the mainland. The lake was now horseshoe-shaped. And shallower than before. The notch in the terminal moraine where the creek flowed out had been scoured from a steep V into a deeper U. Everything else was gone. The blue tent. The azaleas. Most of the trees, except for one massive red fir that now canted steeply downhill with something orange caught high in its branches. Down the canyon the underbrush and trees had been mostly scoured off the face of the earth. Strewn over it all were rocks and sand and broken trunks and branches and the debris and spoils that had once been the moraine. The trail was obliterated. Erased.

There was no sign of a blue tent. No sign of Carla or Bounce. No sign of any life. It must all have been flushed down into the canyon below.

Ernie shivered in the chilly mountain air. Soon an indifferent sun would spill its light and warmth on this altered world as if nothing had happened. A sharp aftershock shook the ground and almost knocked him off his feet. Rocks clattered down the cliff face, some splashing into the water.

He crunched and squished over to his backpack, which still hung from the massive red fir trunk. It had been splashed and knocked askew by the wave, but for the most part was dry inside. Ernie peeled off his wet night shirt and sweat pants and rubbed his goose bumps dry with a towel. From the sopping tent he retrieved the stuff sack that had served as his pillow and drew out his trousers and down sweater. The left arm and right leg were soggy, but the rest had remained dry in the waterproof bag, so he pulled them on. He found his boots and a dry pair of socks in the backpack. That should keep him warm enough until the sun reached the campsite.

Most everything loose had been washed away. The coffee pot was gone. So was the plastic milk jug. And his cup. His camp shoes. His bowl. His walking stick. But down the slope he saw something caught in a crevice between two boulders, which had served as a sort of natural funnel for the flood water. A rock sieve. There he extracted from the debris his spoon and the billy pot and his water bottle and the fire grill and one waterlogged running shoe.

He lowered the food bag, which was still intact. Then he broke off small dead branches from a white fir, snapped them into kindling, and dug out a spare bottle of matches from the emergency kit in a side pocket of his pack. Once he got a fire started, he added a couple of larger pieces of firewood that had caught in the rocks. They were wet outside, but dry within. Soon a nice warming fire was crackling on the steaming ashes of the fire pit. He held his numb fingers over the flames while the water boiled. In the red glow of impending dawn Ernie drank his coffee directly from the billy pot and felt the return of a surreal sense of normalcy.

The sun finally blazed over the eastern rim, warm and welcome. The ominous red had been burnished to a yellow-orange in the rising. More than mere dust is imparting those baleful hues, Ernie thought. Fires must be burning in the Scott Valley to the east. The whole damned world must be on fire. At least that part which had not been drowned in the tsunami or washed away altogether. Drowned or burned or washed away. But not here, in this sunlight, on this ridge overlooking the rearranged lake and devastated valley.

Ernie climbed into his hammock and sat a long time in the sun's warmth. Stunned. Grieved. But no longer feeling guilt. Things happen as they happen. Carla and Bounce had picked their own campsite. Fate. Luck. No one was at fault. No one was to blame. He weighed the horror of it all against the relief he felt that his heart was again functioning properly.

His thoughts drifted to Rosemary, as he had promised himself they would not. Was she alright? Where was she when it struck? Probably in the arms of her new boyfriend. Ernie spat. Let *him* worry about her now.

And he thought about his house, far below on the coastal plain, five miles upriver from the ocean. Wood frame. Perimeter foundation. Maybe it was okay. Maybe not. Maybe it burned to the ground. No way of knowing. Not up here. He was going to lose it anyway. Without a paycheck. Let those greedy bastards at the bank foreclose on the wreckage. He forced the useless speculation out of his mind.

When the coffee was gone, he dragged his sleeping bag out of the tent and wrung it out as best he could and laid it in the sun across the big granite slab. Then he removed his mattress and blue foam pad and other gear and forced the tent back into shape and pulled the stakes and poured out the water and propped the dripping mess over some sunny boulders to dry.

Ernie heated water for a breakfast of oatmeal and apple chips and almonds. The sun had grown too hot for the hammock, so he relocated to a spot in the shade of the red fir and ate on his blue pad leaning against a damp log. He couldn't keep his eyes off the naked white scar in the headwall and the new peninsula jumbled below. As the sun crawled down the headwall face, yellow-red from the east, long fingers of shadow clocked downward. Somewhere on the far shoulder of that half-dome of exposed bedrock lay the Pacific Crest Trail. There it hooked briefly east-west before resuming its rightful trajectory, northward to the east and southward to the west.

The air grew smoky. A gauze curtain was closing, muting the sunlight. It bore not the sweet fragrance of wood smoke, but the stench of burning tar paper. Tar paper and garbage.

Something caught his eye, moving up there on the broken rock face. At first Ernie thought it was a patch of dirty snow. But the snow was all gone. Washed away or covered up. No, this was something moving in the landscape. Something small and white. Something inching its way down on the left side of the precarious new fall of broken talus. Near a notch at the top. Ernie wished he had brought his binoculars.

Someone was climbing down. Slowly. Painstakingly. Descending one sharp cleaver of rock at a time. Ernie couldn't make out whether it was a man or a woman. But it had to be a man. Only a man would be crazy enough to try descending the nearly vertical and unstable talus. If he didn't tumble off, or cut himself on the broken shards, with the next jolt the whole mess could start sliding again and crush him. Ernie wanted to look away, but found he could not.

"*Hello!*" echoed from the lake bowl. The white figure stood atop a massive granite block, waving his arms over his head. Looking across the distance at Ernie.

Ernie stood up and stepped into the sunlight. "*Hello!*" he shouted back, and returned the arm-waving.

"*Are . . . you . . . okay?*" the voice called slowly. The words sailed in surprisingly clear and distinct.

"*Fine!*" Ernie replied, without as much volume as before. "*And you?*"

The distant figure made some sort of gesture that Ernie couldn't make out. "*Later,*" the man hollered, and slowly resumed his precarious descent. He seemed intent on coming Ernie's way. Making contact. Talking it all over. Ernie wasn't sure he welcomed the company.

After a while Ernie climbed down the access path to pump water directly from the lake. The forest of lodgepole pines had been destroyed. Many had been snapped off at ground level. Others were uprooted entirely. A few trees still stood, mostly white fir, canted this way and that by the wave's double punch of surge and retreat. The deadfalls now lay in a jumble of jackstraws across the route. The sweet aroma of pine pitch hung heavy in the air. Ernie counted seventeen trunks he had to climb over or duck under to reach the old shoreline.

The lake level was several feet lower than the evening before, so he had to cross another ten feet of muddy bottom to reach the water. It was murky and shallow. He found a rock that allowed him access to a pool, where he dangled the input hose and carefully pumped full his bottle and pot.

When Ernie looked up, the stranger was circling counterclockwise along the exposed lake bottom toward him. It had taken him more than an hour to reach the bottom of the slide. Ernie left the pot on a flat rock and circled clockwise to meet him.

The newcomer was carrying something over his shoulder. A fishing pole. Just like Bounce. For an instant Ernie's heart leapt. *Could that be Bounce?* But it wasn't. It couldn't have been. He didn't look anything like Bounce. Ernie's imagination was playing tricks.

There was something rough and awkward about the man's gait. Like maybe he had injured his feet. Otherwise he appeared agile and scarecrow thin and a bit younger than Ernie, but not by much. His blond hair was cropped short, making his head seem somehow too narrow. He wore a white T-shirt with a faded logo and blue hiking shorts and a gray sweatshirt tied around his waist. On his bare feet were flip-flops. He carried no backpack. "Got any water?" he called from a hundred feet away.

Ernie held up his bottle and handed it to him as he arrived. "Drink all you want. I can pump more."

The fellow sucked down most of the liter. Wiped his mouth on his arm. "Thanks. That was thirsty work." He stuck out his hand. "I'm Bob. My friends call me 'Slim.'"

"Ernie." Ernie reached out to shake, but Bob intended a fist bump. So Ernie closed his fist for a bump, but Bob opened his for a shake. Suddenly aware that both gestures were out of place, they grinned at each other, and dropped their hands. In awkward silence they sized each other up, two warriors from unknown tribes meeting at a neutral hunting ground.

Finally Ernie asked, "Where're your boots?"

"Gone."

"And your backpack?"

"Gone."

Ernie nodded. This whole earthquake thing was a real fuckaroo. His imagination didn't need a lot of detail. "Could you see anything from up there?"

"The coast," Bob said. "Off to the west. It didn't look good."

"Smoke?"

"Whoa . . . lot's of it. Towers of it . . . black . . . oily . . . spiraling . . . pluming . . . black thunderheads of smoke. Looked like fucking mushroom clouds."

"So . . . this wasn't just some local deal? Just up here in these mountains?"

"Not from the looks of it up on top. No way. Looks like the Big One just clobbered us."

Ernie nodded again. "The triple junction," he muttered. "Cascadia subduction zone." He drew a breath. "Three hundred years in coming."

"Well . . . you better reset your clock. It just came and went."

They stood in silence for a while.

Then Bob asked, "Say, have you got anything to eat? My food pouch was buried under a hell of a lot of rock. Along with everything else."

"So you're all alone?"

"I am now. The rest of my friends're gone. Three of 'em. Whole camp was buried."

"They're all *dead*?"

"Had to be." Bob shuffled his feet. Stared back across the lake. Up to the shattered ridge crest. "I couldn't get to 'em. All that rock." He took a deep breath. "No way anybody could've survived."

"You saw them?"

"Well . . . no . . . not actually . . . ." He grimaced. "All that rock . . . you know . . . but the creek . . . where it crossed the trail . . . ." He squeezed his eyes shut. "The creek . . . was running red."

The image was more than Ernie bargained for. Uneasy, he offered,

"I got some granola bars up at camp. Come on. You can tell me about it up there. If you want to."

They stopped at the shore to pump more water. Bob downed nearly another liter before they refilled the bottle and picked up the full pot. In silence Ernie led the way across the mucky lake bottom and up through maze of splintered timber.

Ernie motioned Bob into the hammock and from his food bag rationed out one granola bar for each of them. He considered his bag of cashews. He coveted those cashews. They were pure energy and meant to last him for eight more days. But a vision of Carla and Bounce played before his eyes. They had given him help freely. Paying it forward. The recollection clouded his parsimony. Plopping down on his mat, he unwound the tie from the bag and set the cashews between them.

Bob helped himself to a big handful.

Ernie sagged against the tree trunk and tried not to obsess about his rations. "Where were you when it hit?" he asked.

Bob considered the question for a long while, as if trying to recollect something that had happened long ago. Straightening things out in his mind. "I was gettin' ready. For an early start. Plannin' t'go fish a little lake up in the rocks. Above where we were camped. The map showed this little no-name lake at the head of the canyon above us. Figured I'd give it a try with first light."

"You were camped in a canyon?"

"A narrow little one. High walls. Right off the trail."

"The PCT?"

"Yeah. It was a little place marked 'Cold Spring' on the map. There was water. This little trickle coming out of the rocks. And a clearing. Just big enough to set up the two tents. I figured the spring was seeping down from that little lake up above. Figured it as surface water. So I filtered mine."

"You must've been up pretty early."

"Oh, I wasn't sleeping anyway. Wanted to check my line. And my pole. Maybe tie some flies. Had to use my headlamp to see a dang thing. And I wanted to check the route. Didn't want to disturb anybody, so I went out to the trail. To the other side of the big boulders. Down the trail a ways, actually. To a saddle. Figured I'd come back for my boots when the sky got brighter. But I got kinda turned around when she started to shake."

Ernie reached over for another handful of cashews, and while he munched he told Bob about Carla and Bounce and their dog Hero and how they were all gone now. And about his heart situation. He concluded, "This was supposed to be my day of rest."

"Well," Bob grunted as he got a firm grip on the cords of the hammock, "even God got a day off." He tugged himself to his feet. "But not me, I guess. I gotta get outa here. All the way. Before it gets dark. I got no sleeping bag. No food. Just this fucking hoodie. And I almost didn't bring it 'cause I thought it was too heavy. Guess I'm gonna have to rest some other day. How's the trail down from here?"

"Wasn't too bad coming in. Just steep. Zig-zags up through a rocky canyon down there. Lot's of switchbacks. Shouldn't be bad, traveling light as you are."

"Okay then," Bob said, glancing around for anything he might have left.

"Unless rock slides have blocked it. But you seem pretty good at climbing down rock slides."

Bob grinned. "Yeah. In flip-flops and all."

"Hey, wait a second. I've got one extra running shoe if you wanna use it. The other one disappeared. Washed away." Ernie found the wet sneaker and handed it to Bob.

"Left foot. Perfect! That's the right foot," he quipped. "Strap on my left sandal's about to break. So the left one's the right one." Bob laced the shoe onto his sockless foot and hobbled back and forth between the boulders, listing a little to the right, getting use to a new gait. "Thanks. This'll make it a hell of a lot easier."

"Wish I had the other one." Ernie bent and pulled a couple of granola bars out of his bag. "Take these along, too. And drink some more water."

"Thanks." Bob swigged down what was left in the bottle.

"I can pump more."

"No," Bob said, "I'm good." He held out the fishing rod and his small tackle bag. "Here. You're gonna need this more than I do."

"No, I couldn't–"

"Sure you can. You can get it all back to me after you get down."

"How'll I find you?"

"Look." Bob unzipped the bag. "My name and address are taped inside."

"Gee, I don't know . . ."

"I'll just leave them here." Bob set the bag on a rock and propped the rod against it.

Neither had anything more to say. There was an unexpected somberness between them. Both felt it. Neither said anything.

"Well, so long." Bob limped down the trail.

"Goodbye." Ernie watched him grow smaller as he circled above the devastated area. Just before disappearing into the canyon defile, Bob found something caught in the manzanita. He turned and waved it over his head, but from that distance Ernie couldn't make out what it might be.

Then he was gone. Bereavement was a cold blade. Ernie drew a deep breath. At least his food would hold out longer this way. Another sharp aftershock punctuated the solitude.

So Ernie busied himself with housekeeping. He shook and turned his sleeping bag. It was still too soon to try fluffing it up. The tent was drying nicely. He repositioned the damp side toward the sun. Item by item he sorted through, inspected, and turned his wet gear. The smoky haze was increasing, blunting the sun's rays, but he remained optimistic that everything would dry by nightfall.

Then he sat down and inventoried his rations. He had no intention of cutting the trip short. No desire to hurry back to that mess he had left down below. It was going to be tight, but everything was going to work out, even if he missed a meal or two before it was over.

He recalled that orange thing he saw hanging over the ruined campsite down below. It required investigation. Maybe it was Carla and Bounce's food bag. And that could be a game changer.

Ernie picked his way down the moraine. Below his camp the trail had been erased. As he approached the outlet notch where Carla and Bounce had camped, the footing grew more scoured and ravaged. Broken timber was strewn far down the canyon or else tossed in piles onto the lake bed by the backwash. The lone standing tree was the huge red fir. It now leaned down canyon. From a sturdy branch hung two fat stuff sacks. The orange one he had spotted that morning. Above it was a smaller, green one. It looked like they had originally been double hung, maybe ten feet off the ground, but were now braided together and twisted around the branch, which had risen up another five feet as the tree tilted away.

He had to climb back up to where undamaged timber still stood higher on the moraine. It took him a lot of tromping through the woods to find a pole ten feet in length, sturdy enough, but not too heavy to wield. He dragged it down the moraine and tried freeing the food bags by poking and prodding at them, this way and that, until his arms grew too weary to hold the pole. It was no use. The bags were so twisted and knotted fifteen feet above his head that he finally gave it up.

Ernie spent most of the afternoon in the hammock, shaded by the two white firs. He ate peanut butter and crackers and dried apple chips and drank a lot of water. He turned his gear in the sun every half hour or so until he could finally shake some fluff back into his down bag. He retrieved more drinking water from the lake. He fiddled with the fishing rod. Ernie wasn't much of a fisherman, but it would be cool to be able to catch some of his own food. He couldn't count on it, though. If there were any fish left in the lake, they would be skittish for a long time to come. Then he took a long, slow stroll down the canyon in search of anything that may have been caught in the brush. Maybe even a dead fish or two. But he found nothing useful.

Ernie cooked another freeze dried dinner over the wood fire and ate directly from the pot. His only vessel. He swung in the hammock, gazing out over the lake, studying the details, fascinated by how the features had been rearranged. Yet how everything now seemed so permanent and immutable, as if the landscape had never been otherwise. The sun dropped behind the western cliffs. His day of rest had passed too swiftly. Ernie yawned and wondered if God felt the same way.

4

"Er-nie!"

The voice seemed to come from far away. Carla's voice. Out of a dream. And then it wasn't. Ernie spun toward it and nearly fell out of the hammock. He must have been dozing. Then he heard the crunch of gravel.

"*I'm baa-ack!*"

Ernie planted his feet on the ground and turned to watch Bob crest the ridge in an exaggerated Groucho Marx glide.

"Notice anything?" Bob asked.

Ernie glared at him, not fully awake. Bob was even skinnier than he remembered. And his head was narrower. But his gait was even. "Yeah. Y'got sneakers on both feet."

"Bingo!"

"Where'd you find the other one?"

"In a bush about a half-mile down. On my way out. That's what I was tryin' to show you." He grimaced. "But I think I'm getting blisters. Got any water?"

Ernie pointed to the half-full bottle perched on a flat rock.

Bob guzzled off what was left and belched. "What's for dinner?"

"Why'd you come back?" Ernie demanded.

"Couldn't get down. Canyon's blocked. Totally. And the slickrock around the sides . . . it can't be climbed. Too damn steep. I almost got myself in a jam a coupla times trying. Way too dangerous. Even with ropes, it would be. And we don't have any ropes. Do we?"

Ernie watched him for a while. Thinking it over. Calculating. Finally he said, "Actually, I don't know. About your dinner. It may be in a couple of bags hanging over the old campsite down there."

Bob climbed the slab and gazed down the hill. He spotted the orange sack. "You couldn't get it down?"

Ernie shook his head.

"You tried?"

Ernie nodded. "Double hung. But all entwined around the branch. Maybe fifteen feet up. Tried poking them down with a pole, but they wouldn't budge. Too wound up."

"Bummer." Bob thought about it. "You got a knife, don't you?"

Ernie drew his six-inch lock-back out of its sheath on his belt and flipped it open.

"And the pole you were using, is it still down there?"

Ernie shrugged. "I guess so."

Bob retrieved his tackle bag from the rock where he had left it. "C'mon. Let's go get us some supper."

They found the pole on the ground where Ernie had dropped it beneath the bags. Bob took the knife and sawed notches in the narrow end, one longitudinal and a couple at right angles, then patiently lashed the knife into the notches with fishing line. He took his time, tying it off with some fishing knots Ernie had never seen.

"That might work," Ernie conceded.

They tested it against the trunk. It seemed solid. Together they hoisted the lance over their heads and were just able to reach the drawstring of the orange bag where it dangled from the tangled rope. Like acrobats performing a tip-toe high-wire dance, they managed to saw through the cord in a few quick stokes, and then scattered as the heavy bag plunged to the earth between them.

"Let's see what we got," Bob said, grinning.

In high spirits they began pulling out the larger items. A bag of tortilla chips. A can of Dinty Moore beef stew. Tuna. A tin of sardines. Beef jerky. A can of marinated herring. A potato. A carrot. Two cans of pork and beans.

"Jesus," Bob wondered, "how long were these folks planning on staying?"

"No idea. But that's a hellofa lotta weight, those cans."

Bob dumped out the rest. Crackers. Two apples. An orange. A fat bag of homemade gorp. Bags of muesli and granola. Three packages of ramen noodles. A stick of melted butter. Salt and pepper shakers. A plastic pint of blackberry brandy.

"How about the stew?" Bob asked, holding up the dented can for inspection.

"Sure. You go ahead. I've already eaten." But Ernie's stomach growled in protest. "Well, I might just have a bite or two. To keep up my reserves."

"We can start with the trail mix, don't y'think?" Bob unwound the tie and scooped a handful out of the bag. Ernie helped himself to a handful too. It was chock full of M&Ms, raisins, and nuts.

The green bag presented a tougher challenge. It was caught a little higher up against the top of the thick branch. They couldn't even see its drawstring or bindings.

"Well?" Ernie asked. "Whaddaya think?"

Bob considered the problem, studied the branch, the bag, the rope, and finally announced, "It's pinata time."

Together they raised the bladed pole and, like golfers, tried a couple of practice swings. Then they counted one, two, *three*, and with one deft slash sliced open the bottom of the bag. Laughing, they jumped back to let rain down chocolate bars and splattering eggs and cheese sticks and a small pink stuff sack and a bag of coffee and a fat plastic bag of kibble.

"The hell's that?" Bob wanted to know, prodding it with his toe.

"Dog food."

"They have a dog?"

"Had. Name was 'Hero.' But let's hang on to it. Just in case things get weird."

Bob snorted. "You mean weirder than they already are?"

"Yeah. Y'never know."

They hauled the booty back to the campsite. Because of the loose items it took two trips. Ernie rebuilt the fire while Bob gathered more dry firewood. Bob cut himself opening the can of stew with the little thumb opener Ernie found in his emergency kit. Ernie dug the Neosporin out of his first aid pouch and applied a band-aid. Bob set the can directly on the grill and watched it until it was bubbling. In the meantime Ernie descended the hill to refill the bottle and the pot with filtered water from the lake.

After dinner Bob helped Ernie set up his tent on the old spot between the fire pit and the big red fir. Ernie shook out the rain fly.

"Think you're gonna need that?" Bob asked, gazing at the hazy, cloudless sky.

"It'll make it warmer inside."

Together they strapped it on. In the gloaming Ernie inserted his air mattress and fluffed up his sleeping bag. He stood up, arched his back to relieve the kinks, and asked, "Where're you planning on sleeping?"

"Is there room in the tent?"

Ernie glared at him.

"It's going to get cold out here. At this altitude. That tent'll be a lot warmer."

This was not what Ernie had planned. He had come up here to get *away* from people. To be by himself for a while. To get his mind straight.

"Remember," Bob added, "I got no sleeping bag."

Whose fault is that? Ernie thought. Yes, it *was* a two-person tent. Nominally, anyway. *His* tent. Perfect for a big guy like himself alone with a little gear. Two people would be crowded. Not to mention the farting and the snoring and the inadvertent touching. But Ernie knew what Carla would have done. He sighed and shook his head. *This is no one's fault.* "I guess we could sleep opposite directions."

"Head-to-feet," Bob grinned.

Ernie nodded and crawled back in and pushed everything over to the right side. It didn't leave a whole lot of room for Bob, but these were hard times, and beggars couldn't be choosers. When he emerged, he asked, "That all you got? Just that hoodie?"

"That's it. Sorry."

Ernie thought it over. "Well . . . here's the deal. I guess I can loan you my sweat pants to sleep in.   And my down sweater. I'll figure something else out for my pillow. Maybe my towel."

"Thanks."

"And I can loan you an extra pair of socks. My air mattress is only four feet long, and I usually put the Thinsulite pad under my legs . . . but I guess you could use that too for the night."

"Thanks."

"Oh . . . and I have one of those emergency blankets . . . somewhere . . . those little silvery things that're supposed to reflect your heat back at you. I guess you could wrap yourself in that for a cover."

"That'll make it warmer. Thanks."

Ernie shrugged. "That's about all I've got to offer."

"That's plenty. Thanks. I owe you."

Ernie waved it away. "We're good."

In front of a blazing fire they watched faint stars begin to fill the hazy sky as the air grew cool. Ernie lounged in the hammock. Bob, in his borrowed night clothes, leaned against the tree on the blue pad. Yawning, Bob volunteered a little about himself. He was an amateur photographer. Worked at a camera shop in Eureka. Yawn. He had just met the woman he hiked in with. At a folk dance at the Bayside Grange. Didn't really know her. Yawn. And the other couple had been friends of hers, not his. He hardly knew them at all. He fell silent.

Grudgingly Ernie reciprocated by recounting the dullness of his work as an accountant. And his disappointment. He had been working part time for Barnes and Decker in Valley West. North Arcata. But when he asked for a reasonable raise, they let him go. Hired a new associate. Full-time. A young bitch who didn't know diddly squat about the fucking tax code. He was still pissed off. Most of the job had been tax preparation. The tax code asked too much of ordinary folks. "You do your own taxes?"

Bob's head had already nodded to his chest. His breathing had grown deep and regular.

"Bob?"

No reply.

"*Bob?*" Ernie barked, more sharply.

"Huh?"

"Hey, man, you were asleep. You better go on to bed. You'll catch cold out here."

Obediently, with a grunt of apology, Bob struggled to his feet, shuffled over to the tent, kicked off his shoes, and crawled inside without another word. Ernie threw in the blue pad and zipped the door closed behind him. Then he puttered around putting the campsite in order, enjoying the solitude. The frogs were croaking again down by the water. As if nothing had happened. He brushed his teeth and peed and lay back in the hammock to wait for the fire to die down to embers. A sliver moon in the west followed the sun down. Through the flickering, fire-lit branches of the great fir overhead, the stars lay faint and dim. Without definition. Unlike the bright pinpoints of the night before. The Milky Way was a dull smudge across the sky.

When the chill reached his bones, Ernie followed Bob into the tent. Bob was curled on his pad, hugging his knees, snoring quietly. The sharp whine of the zipper didn't disturb him. Ernie unfolded the emergency blanket and spread it over him.

5

Ernie was up with first light. A fine black soot encrusted everything. There was no drone of jetliner overhead. No contrails engraved across the brightening sky. No distant throb of helicopters. No traffic noise. No hint of civilization at all. Cold, hazy smoke blunted the mountains and reddened the eastern horizon. As he peed behind the big slab, he muttered to himself, "Wonder what's going on down there?"

"Say what?" Bob mumbled from inside the tent.

"Oh, nothing. Just wondering how they were making out down below. With the fires and all."

"Uh," Bob grunted. Then, after awhile, "You up for good?"

"Yeah. I'll build a fire and heat up some water. You go on back to sleep."

Ernie brushed his teeth, brought down the food bags, and fetched water from the lake while the fire caught. When the water boiled, he made his coffee in the empty Dinty Moore can. He opened both of the cans of pork and beans and set them on the edge of the grill to heat, then retired to the hammock with the bag of gorp and his coffee to wait for the sunrise.

The smell of food finally roused Bob. From inside the tent he asked, "What's that I smell a'cookin', Cookie?"

"Pork and beans."

"The sun up yet?"

"No. Not yet. Soon. How'd you sleep?"

"Okay, I guess. Didn't get too cold, anyhow. Coulda used a thicker mattress, though."

"Well, you should be out of here by tonight."

Bob zipped open the door and stuck out his head. "You're not hiking out too?"

Ernie shook his head. "I'm still planning to make a try for Man Eaten Lake."

Bob stepped out and shivered. "Why?"

Ernie laughed at that. "Why *anything*? Why are we up here sleeping on the ground in the first place?"

Bob shrugged. "Gotta do something."

"Yeah . . . well, I was heading for Man Eaten Lake. *That's* what *I* was doing. Nothing's changed. Not for me, anyway."

Bob dropped down the slope to pee. When he returned, he grabbed a handful of gorp and said, "Got anything I can make coffee in?"

"You can use this. I'm done." Ernie held out the empty stew can. "We'll each have our own after we finish the beans."

They ate pork and beans carefully from the hot cans, Ernie using the only spoon, and Bob drinking and slurping and trying not to burn himself. Then they split an apple and the orange, opened the crackers, and got into the trail mix.

Bob sat back, belched, and asked, "What's the name of that lake of yours again?"

"Man Eaten?"

"Yeah. Funny name. How do you get to it?"

"Well . . . its north of here. Up in the Marbles. Just off the Pacific Crest Trail. All I have to do is get up to the ridge and catch the PCT and walk north until I get there."

Bob nodded. "Guess that's the way I'll be headin' too."

Ernie frowned.

"Not much choice."

"But you'll be dropping back down into the valley."

"Soon as I can find a side trail down." Bob was quiet a moment, then added, "We can split the load. I can carry your backpack until I find a way down. After that you're on your own."

Bob surrendered the sweat pants and down jacket, but Ernie let him keep the extra pair of socks. Together they shook out the tent and folded it and stuffed all the gear into the backpack. Then they dropped down to the lake and pumped water and drank as much as they could hold. The only water they would be able to carry with them was in the single quart bottle.

Bob harnessed himself into the backpack and cinched up the belt. "Jesus, you sure do like to travel heavy."

"Plan to be here awhile." Ernie strapped on the food bag, now bulging with their newfound bounty, and slung the fishing pole and tackle bag over his shoulder. Then he policed the bivouac, sad, as usual, to be moving on. "Guess we got everything . . ."

"And a hell of a lot more!"

". . . so let's get going."

They contoured northward through the sparse trees until they intercepted the trail from the junction below and began a steep plod up toward the ridge crest through a shallow valley of bunchgrass and boulders. The granite sand was spangled with patches of pale blue phlox. With Bob in the lead, they climbed toward a hot sun, haloed in pale yellow, with the taste of stale smoke in their nostrils and on their tongues.

After a few minutes Bob fell into a droning banter which paced their slow steps and deep breathing. "Looks like this . . . trail is still . . . pretty good . . . up here . . . anyway . . . I tried to . . . get up to where . . . we're going . . . you know . . . the morning after . . . the quake hit . . . you know . . . but the PCT . . . was blocked . . . north of where . . . we were camped . . . big fucking slide . . . wiped it out . . . totally . . . couldn't get . . . around it . . . cliff was . . . so steep . . . too steep . . . t'get around . . . couldn't go north . . . couldn't get back . . . south . . . that's why . . . I hadda climb . . . down those nasty . . . fucking rocks . . . you know . . . the one down . . . to your lake . . . remember? . . . man . . . that was sumthin' . . . wasn't it?"

"I don't know," Ernie snapped. The constant yammering was beginning to grate on his nerves. He had always preferred to hike in silence and drink in the solitude of the landscape.

After a while Bob began again. "Hey . . . what was that . . . Carla babe like? . . . the one . . . you were . . . tellin' me about . . . how old . . . d'you think? . . . she was . . . was she . . . good lookin'? . . . I'll bet she . . . had nice legs . . . with all that . . . hiking n'all . . . what was . . . she wearin' . . . anyway? . . . an' how about . . . her boobs?"

The conversation was making Ernie ill-tempered. Something personal and private had been violated. "Let's not . . . talk about . . . *her* . . . okay?" After a few steps, he added, "In fact . . . let's not talk . . . about anything . . . okay?"

They both fell silent. Concentrating on their footsteps. On their breathing. On the phlox. On the twisted shapes of foxtail pines as they crept past. It was a longer climb than they had anticipated, but at last they finally topped the ridge in a grove of gnarled mountain mahogany. The Pacific Crest Trail traced a dusty path along the narrow saddle before rising northward around the shoulder of a bulky peak. They eased off their loads for a breather and a mouthful of precious water.

The crest, where they stood, was a sky island of dirty yellow sunshine. In silence they took in the towers of gray-black smoke pluming southward along the coast in the distant west. Below them to the east the Scott Valley was locked in a heavy black sea of smog.

Ernie shook his head. "You wanna go *down there*?"

"Got to," Bob replied.

Ernie thought about it. "Can't make it south, you say?"

"No way. Big slide down maybe a half mile."

Ernie nodded and turned to eye the trail where it climbed gently northward to enter a shady forest of red fir. "Okay then. Guess we'll be hiking together the other way. You ready for me to carry the backpack?"

"No. I'm good." Bob thought about it, then grinned. "Besides, if you're plannin' on havin' that heart attack of yours up here, I'd rather you did it after we split up."

The going was slow. Fallen trees and slip-outs blocked the trail and required them to detour around, sometimes above, sometimes below, but always across the steep bank where the gravel and rock and cones were loose and slippery. They encountered no stoppers, although a few of the portages required steady nerves and careful teamwork in transferring the backpack and food bags. The real danger lay not in the terrain itself as much as in their unwillingness to turn back.

Late in the afternoon, with the hot sun reflecting doubly from the pale slickrock, they arrived at the Music Creek junction, where Bob had hoped to find a side trail down to the west. But the entire mountainside seemed to have collapsed. Cabin-sized boulders blocked the access trail. They sat on sharp-edged blocks of granite and drained off the last of the water.

"Gotta find more water," Bob said.

Ernie was studying the map. "Looks like there's a big lake right off the trail in a couple of miles. Not more than three. We should be able to make it by nightfall."

"Even at this pace?"

"Yeah."

"If we can make it at all."

"An access trail from the lake drops straight down into the Scott Valley. You can finally bail out."

"If that trail's not blocked."

"Jesus," Ernie gibed, "look who's Mr. Negativity today. We better eat some lunch. That'll pick up your spirits."

"And lighten our loads," Bob grinned. "Good idea. I'm hungry. Let's eat it *all* up . . . and then get the hell outta here."

They rummaged through the bags and set out the heaviest items: the sardines, the tuna, and the marinated herring. They opened all three tins and ate the fish with crackers. In the end, it was difficult to choke down the last few bites without water, but they managed. The saltiness left them thirstier than ever.

The trail was rough and rocky as it descended northward. Soon a small stream flowed across their path from an alpine rock garden with bright pink bitterroot flowers above the trail, and they stopped to refill the water bottle and quench their thirst. Beyond the stream they had to scramble around a mountain hemlock bent low over the trail by winter snows.

They mounted the cliff, where the Pacific Crest Trail had been blasted into the nearly vertical east face of the solid pluton. This was a landscape of towering spires and varnished vertical cleavers and jagged white rock faces utterly inaccessible to the casual cross-country hiker. They came to a place where the trail ledge had been broken out by a falling boulder, leaving a three-foot gap with an abyss below. Beyond the gap was a flat slab, two-feet wide, with a sheer drop-off on the far side where the trail jogged left. They took off their packs. Bob, with a hangdog expression, insisted on turning around and finding another way down. But before he could finish his argument, Ernie had taken a running jump and landed, tottering, on the far side of the gap. He turned and grinned. "Swing my backpack over to me, will you?"

It was a tricky maneuver, but they managed.

"Now toss me the food bags." Bob complied. "And the fishing stuff."

When everything had been transferred, Bob stood at the precipice and shook his head. "I can't do it."

"Don't *think* about it . . . just *do* it."

Bob stood frozen. "I can't."

"Alright then," Ernie said, as he strapped on the backpack. "Have it you own way." Leaving the orange food bag and fishing gear beside the trail, he hoisted his own food bag into his arms and turned. "I'm going. You figure it out for yourself." He plodded along the narrow ledge and around a granitic bulge, where he stopped and waited out of sight. He made room for his food bag in his bulging backpack. No Bob. "Shit," he said to himself. "Okay . . . not my problem." With difficulty he hoisted the heavy backpack, harnessed it on, and continued northward.

Ernie hadn't gone a quarter mile when he heard footsteps behind him. It was Bob, trotting toward him, orange bag and fishing gear bouncing over his shoulders. "I made it," was all he said.

What should have been an easy trek stretched out endlessly in the afternoon heat. Below them the alfalfa fields of the Scott Valley remained hidden in a thick black soup of smog. Then, at the bottom of a long straight trudge, the PCT dipped to cross a substantial creek. It was the outlet stream beneath the lake. Exhausted, they turned up a spur trail and climbed to the northeast shore, dropping their burdens on the lightly forested slope.

South, across the lake, patches of forest filled the gullies. A few renegade trees climbed the steep, white slopes of the bare granite bowl. There were no level campsites where they stood. The north shore sagged southward, and the lake arced west around the forested bulge, which blocked their view of the far end. Above it, in the distance, a white granite massif loomed, peaked by a jagged spire.

They found a good campsite at the northwest corner of the lake beneath the towering headwall. Flat slabs of granite had been stacked together to form a table and chairs. The fire pit was big and clean, and a log had been propped up as a bench. Between the lake and the headwall, past a narrow hedgerow of alders and serviceberry, a broad swath of meadow rose and curved northwest toward a steep canyon. A shallow creek trickled down the green sward from unseen ponds in the rock above. The grass and shrubs were all bent toward them, leaning downhill as if a giant gardener had dragged a fine-toothed rake down the valley floor.

"It flooded here, too," Ernie said. "But not so much. Didn't move the rocks. Or the big trees.”

"Or the high ground,” Bob added. “What’s that?” He pointed to something yellow and blue caught in the thicket. They walked over. It turned out to be a tent, wrapped around the trunk of an aspen. “Somebody’s sliced it open.”

"To get their stuff out,” Ernie agreed. “Somebody was here when the earthquake hit.”

"An’ it looks like they survived.”

"And they got out.”

6

They sipped blackberry brandy as the water boiled for the ramen noodles. Bob walked out to explore the brushy side trail down to the Scott Valley. Ernie cut up the potato and carrot and added them to the soup. While it simmered, he erected the tent and inserted the things they would need for the night. He hung the backpack on a spike in an old hemlock. When Bob returned, they passed the bottle and sat on a log to eat the soup and tortilla chips, Ernie out of the pot and Bob from the old stew can. Darkness fell over them. When the brandy was gone, Ernie dug a pint of Yukon Jack out of his pack.

After the dishes were done and the food hung and the campsite put in order, they sat in front of the blazing fire and sipped the sweet whiskey. Ernie in his hammock. Bob on the blue pad propped against a fallen log. Warm. Bellies full. At peace with the world.

Bob was the first to break the silence. He talked of many things. About backpacking. About other places he had seen. About what he hoped to do when he got down. About life in general.

Ernie ignored much of the palaver. He was content with his own thoughts. His heart was pumping regularly. The food bag was full. And he would have plenty of time for silence after Bob left.

"What was the name of that lake again?” Bob asked.

"Which one?”

"The one you’re hiking to.”

"Man Eaten Lake. Jesus Christ! How many times do I have t’tell you?”

"What does that mean, anyway?"

"What?"

"'Man Eaten.'"

Ernie thought about it. "How the hell do *I* know what it means?"

"Well, you're the one who's going there."

"Yeah, but I don't have to know what the goddamn name means. Pass the bottle."

"But you're *going there*. See what I mean? Here."

Ernie took a big gulp. "No, I don't see what you mean."

"The name doesn't make any sense."

"Okay. So what?"

"Well . . . maybe you shouldn't be goin' there."

"Bullshit. What difference does the stupid *name* make?"

Neither said anything for a while. Then Bob added, "Anyway, I don't like the sound of it. You shouldn't go there."

"Well, *you* don't have to fucking go there. Alright? But don't tell *me* what to do. Just leave me alone."

They brooded in silence as the bottle passed back and forth a few more times and the frogs began their chorus down beside the water. Ernie got up and threw a couple more branches on the fire.

"Hey, Ernie?"

"Yeah? What?"

"Something I'd like to ask you," Bob said.

"What?"

"Were you really plannin' on leavin' me back there? On that ledge?"

"I *did* leave you there."

"Yeah . . . but *why*?"

"I knew you'd figure it out by yourself."

"But . . . you left the food and fishing rod on your side."

"A little motivation. For you to do the right thing. Here, have another sip."

Bob took the bottle and tipped it. "No . . . no, that's not it." He sat in silence. "You really didn't give a shit about what happened to me."

"Jesus!," Ernie snapped. "I'm not your keeper. You're a big boy. Let's just not talk about it any more."

They sat in silence for a while, staring into the flames. Then Bob said, "Somethin' else."

"Uh? What now?"

"It's kinda personal."

Ernie sighed. "Okay. I'll bite, if you pass the bottle. What's buggin' you?"

"No offense, but . . . well . . . it's just . . . how come you're so . . . so fucking *mean*?"

"Mean?"

"Yeah . . . like, sour. Nasty. Grumpy. Your mother drop you on your head when you were a baby?"

Ernie had never thought of himself like that. "I . . . I just like my privacy is all. My personal space. My solitude. That's why I come up here in the first place."

Bob considered the response, then shook his head. "But it's more'n that. You just don't seem to . . . to give a damn . . . about anybody else. About what's happening down there. To those folks down there. In Etna, for example."

Ernie took a long swig. "I care."

"Then why don't you want to get down there and help out."

Ernie drew a deep breath. "Actually, that's sort of a long story. Those 'folks down there,' as you call 'em, haven't been very nice to *me*."

Bob waited to hear him out.

So Ernie started talking. About himself. About his life. Something he never did. Ever. And once he started, it was like punching a hole in a dam. The stories gushed. He told Bob about his job and how he hated it and how he had lost it. About how the bank was foreclosing on the house he was now sure to lose. When he came to Rosemary, he couldn't stop. In excruciating detail he laid out the whole ugly romance and the infidelities and the final horror of losing her to another man. Her fucking Pilates instructor, of all the worthless creeps she might have fallen for. And then came the heart arrhythmia on the way up to the lake. Another bad deal. He could die at any minute. His throat was tight and his chest heaved and tears were rolling down his cheeks by the time he finally stopped.

The camp grew quiet. The fire crackled. Frogs croaked down by the lake. Overhead, indifferent stars burned indifferently in the blackened sky.

"Okay," Bob said at last. "And I bet your fucking dog died, too."

Ernie stared at him, bewildered. "What dog?" Then he got it. "You think this is *funny*," he sputtered. "This isn't funny!" But he started laughing. He couldn't help it. Bob laughed too, and they fed off each other. They laughed so hard they doubled over and gasped for breath. "*Your fucking dog died!*" Ernie guffawed, and they both howled with laughter until they were totally spent.

7

Ernie woke up to the sound of the tent zipper opening and closing. There was movement outside the tent. Then all grew still and he went back to sleep. When he awoke again the sun was already on the tent. Groggily he crept out into the crisp morning air. Bob was nowhere to be seen. Probably up in the meadow digging a hole for himself, he figured. But when he looked around, he saw his sweat pants, down jacket, and extra pair of socks folded neatly on the blue pad on a fallen log. The running shoes were gone, as were the fishing pole and tackle bag. "Shit," Ernie muttered with a coated tongue, "he coulda kept the fucking socks."

Alone again, Ernie drew a deep breath and fought back an urge to cry. *Not so much as a fare thee well*, he thought. *Oh well, he'll probably be back when he finds the trail blocked.*

But Bob didn't come back, and Ernie busied himself with breakfast and his own trek onward to Man Eaten Lake. Somehow much of the urgency was gone. *Why am I going there?* he truly wondered for the first time he could remember.

He found he had too much food to carry, so he left the excess in the green bag hanging from a branch of the old hemlock. And the socks, too, in case Bob came back. He filled his water bottle and drank down as much as he could hold, then started northward on the PCT. The pack was still heavy, but he felt light. Lighter than he had in years. His pace was unhurried and steady. After a couple of miles he crossed a narrow saddle with a large lake below at the bottom of a steep rock slide. *Bob could have made it down there*, he thought. Then he climbed onto a vast cirque of granite slickrock into which the trail had been blasted, and soon passed above a smaller lake, a little gem glimmering turquoise in its stark white bowl far below. Beyond the lake the PCT continued to climb the stark east face until it swung westward onto the forested north slope and followed the ridge crest down through changing scenery. The lush forests and white granite gave way to sparse stands of stunted trees growing out of gnarly red rock, black inside where broken open. It seemed to Ernie an alien landscape.

He talked to Bob. Even though Bob wasn't there. He talked to him in his mind. He pointed out a particularly gnarly tree. And the way the sun glistened off the surface of the strange green rock. And he laughed again, like he had the night before. *I bet your fucking dog died!* Bob had led him out of a maze. *It's all a joke.*

The Russian Wilderness ended where the trail intercepted the Sawyers Bar-Etna Road at Etna Summit. Directly across the dirty swath of two-lane blacktop he saw a signpost where the PCT continued, destined for the Marble Mountain Wilderness to the north. Where Man Eaten Lake waited for him like a malevolent need.

Down the road from the crossing was a small gravel parking lot with neither sign board nor water spout nor toilet. A single dust-coated Subaru Outback gleamed dully in the bright sunlight. The vehicle wore Oregon license plates and a Rogue River Community College decal on the back window. Curious, Ernie wiped away the dust from the passenger side window with his sleeve and peered inside. There was nothing much there. A cup. A sweatshirt. A map. A folded towel. An empty dog bowl. Then his eyes were drawn to the floor behind the driver's seat, where a worn leather basketball rested.

"*Jesus!*" Ernie staggered back, heart pounding, and wobbled for a moment in the hot sun.

I am alive, he thought, as if the notion had never properly occurred to him before. He turned to glare at the trailhead across the road. All those obligations seemed to loosen and slip from his shoulders. And the anger fell away with them like molting scales. *I am alive.* He turned away, cinched up his backpack, and with a new certainty in his step, started down the highway toward Etna.

Mrs. Wigmore's Troops

Mrs. Wigmore smiled as she watched the children at play. With the old feather-duster forgotten in her hand, she gazed out through the tall schoolhouse windows. She was stout and dowdy with a graying bun of wavy brown hair pinned severely against the back of her head. A war widow, like so many others. But today she was smiling. She loved these children, one and all. And she loved the pandemonium of recess, where they explored who they were and what they were capable of and what they might become.

She grew aware of the antique clock ticking on the wall behind her and sighed. Time was short enough for them as children. Soon it would be their time. She returned the duster to its place and stepped out onto the porch.

To the untrained eye it was chaos. A group of younger boys and girls ran and leaped and circled and laughed, lost in a game of their own imagination. Teddy Lawrence, a fourth grader, launched the lopsided basketball with all his might toward the impossibly high netless goal, but it clanged off the rusty metal backboard and refused to drop in, while his cousin Sidney Whithers, a year younger but already a better shot, laughed and jumped from foot to foot as he waited his turn. Three little second-graders in brightly-colored print dresses screamed and laughed as they played follow-the-leader round and round the patch of red and yellow roses, expressing the joy of being flowers themselves. Tim McCullock, a usually-sullen eighth-grader, was trying to impress Molly Sullivan, a year his junior, with his frisbee skills, but he zinged the wobbling disk into the ground at her feet, where it rolled away and they both gave chase.

Mrs. Wigmore picked up the iron rod and ran it around the clanging triangle by the door. Recess was over. Time to return them to order.

The children filed past into the one-room schoolhouse as she counted an even twenty. A score in her charge. They returned to their seats, assigned by age and grade, and settled themselves into the small inkwell desks for the smaller ones and the oak chairs at the oak tables for the older. It would take them a few moments to settle back into silence.

"Now children," Mrs. Wigmore announced, "it's time for your math lessons. Today the second graders will teach the first graders the addition and subtraction tables. Over here." She pointed to desks on her left. "The fourth graders will continue multiplication and division with the third graders. Over there." She pointed to desks on her right. "And the seventh graders will work with the fifth and sixth graders on geometry. In back at the tables. Tim and Otis and Molly, you will work with me on algebra at the back corner table. Is all that clear?"

"Yes Mrs. Wigmore," came the chorus.

"Good. And remember what I always tell you, '*You don't really know it . . . until you can show it.*'"

They chanted the phrase back to her, then broke up into their respective groups.

She handed out the algebra books, and as she helped the three students find the proper exercise, she heard a rolling rumble that sounded like thunder. Far to the west a tower of black smoke was rising into the cloudless sky. The others had heard it too. And their faces were turned toward the rising smoke. Before she could decide what to do, the fire siren from town cut the air. From behind them to the southeast. Three long blasts separated by two short ones.

"Oh dear," said Mrs. Wigmore to herself. "They're coming."

She rose and stepped behind her desk and faced the class, looking more assured than she felt. "Children, please put away your books for now and assemble at the front of the classroom. Like you've done before. It appears as if we are going to have to push the red button again."

There was a moment of shocked silence, then murmurs of unhappiness, especially from the youngest ones, as they all prepared to line up. Four of the older boys slid the desks aside to make room.

Meanwhile Mrs. Wigmore had stepped to the thing in the blind corner of the room behind her desk. Calmly she drew back the olive drab drape to reveal an olive drab machine the size and shape of a small refrigerator. At the top were stenciled in black letters:

RESOURCES MANAGER
Model RM017

The unit had come to life and displayed a pulsing red light. A spiraling hum rose steadily in pitch like the engine of a diesel locomotive warming up. Flashing on a small screen at the center was the word "RECEIV-ING." Below it was a large red button the size of a small fist. Twin green pipes as big as a child's arm rose from the top of the unit, passed through a ceiling thimble, and disappeared into the attic above.

Mrs. Wigmore pulled out the bobby pins and shook down her hair. With her fingers and palms she curried the unruly waves as best she could. Then she slipped on a sort of steel-mesh helmet, green with a single red-tipped antenna poking up in front. The mesh, she was told, would block out the local signal. The antenna would provide her with a higher-phase cancelling signal. Someone had to stay and mind the store.

The machine now flashed "PROCESSING."

She turned to face the class. "Is everyone ready?"

"I don' wanna," whimpered Ricky Sanders, a slender, blue-eyed first grader. "I don' like it!"

"We all have to do our part, Ricky," she admonished. "Even if we don't like it."

"But I gotta go to the bathroom!"

"That can wait until later."

Little Lucy Mendoza began crying softly. Mrs. Wigmore motioned to her older sister, Rosa, who stepped around and knelt beside her, wrapping her arm around the quivering shoulders.

Mrs. Wigmore turned back to the machine. The red light had stopped pulsing. The screen now displayed a constant "READY."

"Now children . . . all together . . . let us unify and breathe to-gether." She drew an exaggerated breath and blew it out. Then another. She stepped over to the machine, as she had done a dozen times before. Except that this time her heart was pounding. This time it was for real. Slowly she raised her hand and held it over the red button. "Now children . . . all together . . . recite with me . . . *I pledge allegiance . . . to the flag . . .*" She punched the button with the heel of her hand.

The spiraling whine exploded upward. An antenna in the bell steeple atop the roof crackled and sparked. Electricity lifted the hairs on twenty heads below, making them stand out comically. Only no one laughed. No. The children had snapped to attention, soldiers now, each receiving his or her own orders. They fell into an orderly formation, and one by one, rank and file, they marched into the old cloak room in the back, which now served as the armory. No Marine Corps drill team ever performed with greater precision. There they pulled on their camo overalls and strapped on their kevlar vests and armed themselves with their assigned weapons, which were sized to fit their varying weights and strengths. And of course they all helped themselves to live ammunition.

They filed outside and took up positions behind concrete highway barriers which had long ago been placed in and about the school and surrounding shrubs. Each deployed in precisely the correct position and posture. Silently they waited, vigilant, weapons loaded and ready. The staccato rattle of automatic fire arose from ahead to the west. An explosion jarred them. Black smoke rose nearby to the south. Tracer bullets whined past and thudded into the wall of the schoolhouse. One shattered a window. But they held their positions.

Suddenly Teddy Lawrence was spun over backwards by the blow of a bullet. He struggled back into position, his left arm dangling uselessly and streaming blood into the grass as he tried to regrip his weapon with just his right hand.

"*Nineteen now,*" Mrs. Wigmore grieved silently from behind the shattered window.

And then, through the rising smoke, the enemy appeared, climbing steadily toward them from the wheatfield below. Without spoken command they each took aim at an approaching figure, no two weapons targeting the same soldier. And they waited. In silence. Teddy Lawrence slumped unconscious at his position, and Molly Sullivan silently acquired his target.

And they waited.

And the enemy advanced, firing wildly.

And they held their fire until the enemy was almost upon them.

Then, in perfect unison, the good little soldiers opened fire with a devastating barrage of death.

Barriers

He slogged through loose desert sand and silt, following the old path that led home. There were other routes, of course, more convenient and faster, but Jacob Ramirez had chosen this way as a symbolic return to his origins. As the closing of a circle. Perhaps even as the completion of a poem. For this was the path he had taken when he left.

He had no difficulty finding his way, though he was returning for the first time in years. His feet still recognized the track through the ancient landscape of his youth. The sandy swales. The scrambles down and up little caliche ravines. The gravel piedmonts, shiny with desert varnish, where the footing was firm. The particular mesquite grove where the course turned south. Then the familiar old saguaro, miraculously still standing, whose broken arm still reached down as if in greeting to an old friend. And at last the artesian pond, surrounded by willows, where the ancient, half-dead cottonwood had not fallen, but still spread its branches over the sky-blue water.

Jacob paused to reminisce and drink from one of the plastic water bottles in his backpack. He and his brother had spent many hours here. But those special days were now long past. Things had changed irreversibly. Jacob slung his pack over his shoulder and began the slow ascent up the shallow draw between ridges festooned with greasewood and cactus, anticipating his first long view southward.

At the crest he stopped and stared at the dull reddish scar off in the shimmering distance. It had not been there the last time he passed this way. He lifted off his sombrero and wiped his forehead with a shirt sleeve. A blinding sun blazed down on his shoulders and bare head, magnifying the sense of irreality. Not quite believing it to be real, he shuffled his sneakered feet through another kilometer of burning white sand until they crunched at last across a new gravel road. His hand reached out and touched the hot, ferruginous structure.

Hollow square steel posts, ten inches in cross section, had been rammed deep into the earth and filled with concrete. They sprouted every five feet, alternating in height between five and six feet. A single heavy railroad track rail had been welded to the north side of the posts, with periodic expansion joints, to prevent passage of any vehicle. The posts had already weathered to a rusty reddish brown. Three taut strands of shiny new barbed wire stood off the dragons-tooth barrier to discourage pedestrian and cow.

A hundred feet beyond, paralleling the barrier, a new barbed wire fence had been erected on white metal posts with a white metal cap pipe to define the international boundary and further impede the progress of cows and humans. Between lay a no-man's land of undisturbed desert. The twin obstructions stretched east and west in dead-straight lines that would never meet, through the mesquite and greasewood, dropping into distant dips and climbing the rolling foothills as far as his eyes could see. They appeared to be a modern-day Maginot Line, and were probably no more effective. Altogether, this new swath of quick-and-dirty industrial construction stunned him as an ugly monument to American insensitivity and misunderstanding.

Jacob shook his head and pressed his fingers against the hot metal rail. This thing was an abomination. Its rusting straight line was a scab. The male force had sliced into the desert's rounded mounds and pliant shrubs as a razor cuts into the belly of the female. A grackle perched on a post, laughing, and hawks soared indifferently overhead. The tortoise would hardly notice the barrier as he crawled beneath it. The mountain lion and bobcat and javelina would slither between the strands of barbed wire. He wondered what the wise coyote would make of such foolishness.

Jacob thought back to the ejido where he grew up. He and his brother had never paid much attention to the old, broken-down barbed-wire fence which split the reservation in two like a dull knife, severing north from south. Those political boundaries were of no consequence to the people living there. In school he had learned that the 1853 Gadsden Purchase had brought Papago lands into the United States, but by its terms the United States agreed to honor all land rights of the area held by Mexican citizens, which included indigenous people. But such imaginary lines had little reality here in the heart of the desert. They were conceived and negotiated and agreed to and paid for by others, far away, who had never set foot among the People of the Desert. His people enjoyed a common history and culture, a common language, and a deep respect for the land and its many sacred places. The Tohono O'odham were one and indivisible. They could not be cloven in two by a rickety old rusting fence.

Until this.

He set down his pack and drank deeply, emptying one water bottle, as he considered his options. He was born on this side of the imaginary boundary line. He had an Arizona birth certificate to prove it. Thus, he was a U.S. citizen. Unlike his brother. Franklin had been born on the other side, after the family moved to the village a few miles south so his father could find work. There, in that little farming community, they had both been raised.

But Jacob *was* a U.S. citizen. And as such he had a right to slip through this ridiculous vehicle barrier and walk right over to the international boundary fence. He would still be within the United States. There were no warning signs prohibiting him from entering the enclosure. And once he had crossed it, if he just happened to climb over the boundary fence, well, then he would become a Mexican problem, and of no further concern to the Border Patrol. Wasn't that right? It made sense to him. And besides, there was no one around to see him.

Jacob took his time surveying his surroundings, then kicked his backpack under the bottom strand of barbed wire. He glanced around again, but saw nothing but a white-tailed rabbit dodging through the creosote bush. It was not too difficult stepping over the lowest strand while bending beneath the heavy rail, but he did manage to catch a barb and tear his new khaki trousers. "Damn," he muttered, probing the flesh beneath the tiny rip. At least the barb had drawn no blood.

Once on the other side, he straightened up slowly, a bit lightheaded from the heat and glare. Cautiously he crossed toward the second fence. Beyond it lay an entirely different culture, spread out like a brushy carpet across a broad basin to the foot of distant, but familiar, mountains. He paused to see if he could recognize any landmarks. With an almost magnetic allure the shallow valley tugged at his memory and his upbeating heart. The only thing moving was the speck of an overloaded hay truck crawling down an invisible road in the glistening distance.

Maybe it was the intense brightness, or the desert heat, or the way the creosote bush shimmered in the breeze that made Jacob feel disoriented. As if an electric current were passing through his mind. He was suddenly unhinged. Disconnected from reality. From *three* realities, actually. Realities that opened around him in vivid clarity, rooted in the three languages that divided his mind. Temporally and physically, each reality was sovereign in its own memories and desires. The feeling was almost auditory, like a choir of angelic music drawing him forth. Spread out before him lay two cultures, the Native American and the Mexican, each hopelessly intertwined and embedded in his past. And behind him, in a strange convergence of recent past and present, there loomed a harsh, rectilinear, male culture that he now dreaded to turn and face.

Oh, yes, these are barriers too, he thought.

Invisible barriers.

Inside my mind.

The roar and rattle of a truck startled him. Jacob turned to see a white pickup plummeting down the gravel road at the head of a thick rooster tail of dust. The vehicle was white like the dust that exploded from beneath its wheels. "Border Patrol" was stenciled boldly below the light bar on the side of the steel detainment shell. To Jacob the speed seemed excessive for the conditions. The truck slalomed and fishtailed in the loose gravel before skidding to a stop with its nose a foot from the barrier. Jacob was impressed with the driver's skill.

Out sprang the driver and stepped quickly to the fence. To his surprise, the figure in the gray-green uniform was a woman. She was tall and bulky above with a short blond ponytail poking out the back of her Border Patrol baseball cap. She withdrew a small black automatic pistol from its holster and pointed it skyway as she called to Jacob, "Sir, stop right where you are."

Her partner, older and less agile, was a heavy fellow with a weathered, lopsided face and brown hair beginning to gray at the temples. He too had withdrawn a pistol from the holster on his belt and was pointing it at the ground. The incongruity struck Jacob. What was supposed to be the standard operating procedure here? Point your gun into the air, or at the ground. For no good reason he suspected the man to be wrong. Not that it made any difference, under the circumstances.

"Sir, raise you hands over your head," called the young woman with careful articulation, so that there could be no misunderstanding.

Jacob studied her, and then her partner, and then he turned to the barbed wire border fence only a few yards away, calculating his chances of making it over before they could reach him. He concluded that he probably could. But the firearms muddled the equation. He doubted they would actually shoot at him. But they could. They could shoot him dead as he climbed over. Or even after he was on the other side.

So Jacob sighed and turned back to face the agents, holding his hands out to his sides. "What do you want with me?" he yelled.

She faced a confused young man, dressed in a black shirt and khaki pants, caught in the restricted area between the two barriers like a deer in headlights. Beneath his tattered straw Mexican sombrero, unkempt black hair spilled down his forehead and over his ears. His cheeks were as round as a rabbit's and covered with a bristle of short black whiskers. A pair of black-rimmed spectacles bisected his face like a bandit's mask and imparted a comical, nerdy appearance. His stubby nose was a bright brown triangle, and his narrow mouth turned downward in what appeared to be a perpetual pout. Though the impression was of roundness, his stout legs and arms appeared solid, not flabby. He was obviously conflicted, and the last thing she wanted was for him to run.

She gave him her warmest smile and repeated as pleasantly as she could, "Please place your backpack on the ground and raise your hands over your head."

Jacob stared at her for a while longer, then removed his backpack from over his shoulder and set it by his feet. He raised his hands.

"Now walk towards me." she instructed. "Slowly."

Jacob glanced down at his pack.

"You can leave your pack where it is."

Jacob began moving slowly toward her. She holstered her gun and performed a quick little acrobatic twist that brought her inside the no-man's land. She sidled to meet him in a roundabout loop, keeping clear of her partner's line of fire. The male agent just stood there with his pistol pointed down and a silly grin on his face.

"Nice trick," Jacob smiled as she approached. "They teach you that in Border Patrol school?"

"Keep your hands over your head," she said, all business. "Now remain where you are while I retrieve your backpack."

Jacob complied, following her with his eyes. She was attractive, with clear skin and wide-set eyes, probably in her late twenties. The bulky appearance of her upper body came from a bullet-proof vest.

She squatted down and zipped open his pack, rummaging through his water bottles, clean underwear, notebooks, and toiletries, then returned everything to the bag and walked back to him. She set his backpack on the ground behind her. "Sir, I'm going to pat you down for weapons now." She withdrew a pair of white latex gloves from a pouch on her belt and pulled them on. "Is that alright with you, sir."

"Sure. No problem."

"Spread your feet please, sir."

Jacob complied. Her hands were expert and quick, and Jacob didn't mind her touching him at all. Up close, tiny creases at the edges of her eyes made him rethink her age. Probably mid-thirties.

"What's this?" she asked.

"Cell phone."

"And this?"

"My wallet."

"Please take them out of your pockets and place them on the ground."

Jacob followed her instructions. When she was finished, she straightened up and called over to her partner, "He's clean, sir." Then she turned back to Jacob. "Can I see some identification, sir?"

"It's in my wallet."

"You can pick up your wallet and phone now."

Jacob flipped through his thin wallet and handed over his Arizona driver's licence.

She inspected it, but did not hand it back.

The male agent yelled over to him with what sounded to Jacob like an east coast accent, maybe New Jersey, "You an Indian?"

"Actually, I'm a citizen of the United States of America," Jacob called back.

"Ya look like a fuckin' Papago t' me."

"I am a member of the Tohono O'odham Nation, if that's what you mean," Jacob responded. He had taken an immediate dislike to the man. "We changed our name back in 1986. But maybe you weren't paying much attention back then."

"Smart ass," grumbled the agent. "Bring 'im back over this side, Gwen. Let's see just how smart this guy is."

She walked him back and showed him the twist move that got him through to the north of the barrier. Jacob felt he had learned something for the day.

The male agent wore the same gray-green uniform as his partner, but without the flak jacket. It looked a whole lot better on her. His was rumpled and had a single silver bar on the collar. They both wore U.S. Customs and Border Protection patches on their shoulders. His name tape read "Nomellini, T. I."

"What's your name?" Nomellini growled.

"Jacob Ramirez." The female agent wrote it down in her notebook.

Nomellini compared the name to the driver's licence he had just been handed. "You got a passport?"

"Not with me," replied Jacob. "Never thought I needed one as long as I stayed inside the country."

"Where were ya born."

"Where?"

"Yeah. *Where?*"

"Not far from here. The village no longer has a name. But it was north of the border. I have an Arizona birth certificate."

"With ya?"

"No."

"What was your business crossin' inta the United States."

Jacob laughed. "I wasn't crossing *into* the United States. I was thinking of crossing *out* of the United States. Into Mexico. But I didn't do it."

Nomellini smirked. "Can ya prove that?"

Jacob considered. "Probably. I have a friend who dropped me off on the trail this morning."

"What's 'is name?"

"Laurie McDougal."

"A lady, huh?"

"Yes." He thought of adding "sir," but just couldn't bring himself to do it.

"Sounds Irish. She your girlfriend?"

"An associate."

Nomellini smirked. "Zat what you call 'em now? What's a white girl see in a fat Papago like you?"

Jacob held his tongue.

"Where's she live?"

"Saguarito."

"Address?"

Jacob recited an address and telephone number, slowly to make sure the female agent got it down correctly.

"Zat where you live?"

"No. I live in Tucson. My address is on my driver's licence."

"What d'ya do for a livin'?"

Jacob hesitated, then told him the truth. "I'm a poet."

"A what?"

"A poet."

"A *poet*?"

"That's right."

Nomellini snorted and turned to his partner. "Ya hear that? Guy thinks he's a fuckin' *poet*? Does it for a *livin'*."

She remained silent, eyes cast on her boots.

Without prompting, Jacob added, "I earn my living writing and publishing books of poetry. You can look me up on the internet. I've got some pretty good reviews. It's what I do for a living. Therefore, I'm a poet."

Nomellini glowered. "How long ya been in the U.S.?"

"I was born here."

"Ever been south a the border?"

Jacob considered his response. "I grew up there . . . on Indian land . . . about five kilometers south of here . . . until I went away to high school in Sells . . . then I was awarded a scholarship to the University of Arizona . . . and I've been living and working here ever since I graduated."

"Why're ya back?"

"Back . . . ?"

"Don't play stupid. You said you were headin' back t' Mexico."

"Oh." Jacob wondered whether it was any of his damned business, but decided this was not a fight he could win. "Because my younger brother is dying of cancer."

"What's 'is name." Not a hint of sympathy.

"Franklin."

"Franklin? First name or last?"

"His given name. First."

"Franklin what?"

"Ramirez. Like me."

"You a Mexican citizen?"

"No, I just told you, I'm a U.S. citizen."

Nomellini glared at him, but couldn't think of anything more to ask. He led his partner a few steps away. There was no attempt to keep Jacob from hearing. "Well, whaddaya think we oughta do with 'im?"

She thought about it for a while. Shrugged. "I say we let him go."

"Humph. I don' know. I think we oughta hold onto 'im for a while. Check out 'is story."

"Save us a lotta paperwork if we let him walk."

Nomellini nodded. Considered the problem. "Yeah . . . but 'e's a smart ass. I don't like his fuckin' attitude."

She shrugged. "No evidence of criminal activity."

"I don't *like* 'im. Fuckin' poet. *Come on!* Acts like he's better'n us. An' he's just a fat little fuckin' Indian."

She said nothing.

Nomellini continued, "I say let's hold 'im under the FSDC. Use it or lose it. It'll teach 'im a lesson an' we'll get 'im outta our hair. Very little paperwork that way."

"He says he's a U.S. citizen."

"Don't matter. What you have ta understand, Gwen, is ya can't be a fuckin' bleeding' heart out here. If ya learn anything from me, it's that part of our job is ta inflict a little pain on these greasers. So they can take the message back to the other greasers. We don't want 'em here."

His partner nodded. "Whatever you say, sir. You're the instructor."

"Bet you ass." He gave it some more thought, then said, "Okay, let's do it. Go ahead and cuff 'im"

She turned to Jacob. "Sir, turn around and put your hands behind your back."

"Is this really necessary?" he protested. "I'm a U.S. citizen!"

"Sir, please put your hands behind your back and turn around," she repeated more forcefully, while Nomellini just watched.

Jacob turned around, and she deftly affixed disposable zip ties to his wrists.

Nomellini stepped over to inspect, slipping a finger under the restraints. "Could have been a little tighter," he said.

"Sorry, sir," she replied. "You want me to take them off and do it again?"

"Naw. He's just a fuckin' Papago." He smirked. "What's a *poet* gonna do? Go ahead and take your vest off. I'll call it in." He headed for the cab of the truck with Jacob's driver's license in hand.

Defeated, Jacob watched as she unzipped her kevlar vest. Sweat stained the arm pits of her uniform. Her neck glistened with perspiration. He read her name tape.

"Moody," he said.

She nodded, then turned and carried her vest and his backpack over to the truck, stowing them behind the front seat. The radio crackled and Nomellini seemed to be arguing with someone.

When she returned, Jacob asked, "Is he your commanding office?"

In a hushed voice she said, "Training officer."

Jacob thought about it. "Well . . . don't let him train away your humanity."

She looked up with a sad smile, her head dipping slightly in acknowledgment. This was not easy for her either.

"Thanks for trying anyway, Moody," he said.

"Not my call." They stood about the same height. Five-ten, he guessed. Eyes at the same level. Hers were a striking pale-gray blue. "And I'm sorry about your brother," she added softly. "But I think you should be out in plenty of time to see him. Soon as your story is verified. Doesn't look like you've broken any laws. Not yet, anyway. But I am going to advise you, next time you should cross at an official port of entry. Okay? Nogales. Or maybe Lukeville."

Jacob dropped his gaze and shuffled his feet. "What's this FS . . . FSC . . . something, he was talking about?"

"FSDC?"

"Yeah."

"Federal-State Detention Compact," she explained. "You're going to a county jail rather than a federal detention facility. We're kind of overcrowded right now."

Jacob wanted to ask her more, but Nomellini shuffled back with a grin on his lopsided face. "We're good ta go. Santa Cruz and Pima are all full up, but they found room for 'im up in Graham County."

"Graham County? So we'll have to transport him all the way up to Safford?"

"No way. We'll drop 'im off at Sells and the van'll take him on down to Nogales. Sheriff'll have a bus there t'take him the rest of the way. He's their problem after we drop 'im. Have ya read 'im 'is rights?"

"I was waiting to see what you found out."

"Okay. Go ahead an' do it then."

Jacob tried to catch her eye, but Agent Moody was already pulling a laminated plastic card out of her cargo pocket. Without looking up she read him his Miranda rights. All about having the right to remain silent. The right against self-incrimination. The right to an attorney or to have one appointed. Jacob barely listened. He knew it already from the television shows.

When she was done, Jacob turned to Nomellini and asked, "Weren't you supposed to read me that before you questioned me?"

"We did," Nomellini snapped without missing a beat. He turned to Moody. "Make sure ya show it that way in your report." Then he wheeled back on Jacob, smirking. "You're under arrest, smart ass."

2

This had been the worst day of his life. Jacob tried to put the horror and the injustice out of his mind, but thoughts of it all kept swirling back, stirring up vivid images and recalling sensations. He couldn't help himself from reliving it all as he dangled his feet over the edge of a top bunk. He gazed around for diversion. Everything seemed a foul-smelling orange. Not really orange. But it all *felt* orange, like the jumpsuits they wore. There were thirteen of them, and the pecking order had been established long before he arrived. Jacob was at the bottom, scarcely worth acknowledging. And that suited him just fine.

He was in a holding cell with no bars and no windows. The barriers here were just four concrete block walls, painted a dirty dull sand color, and a gray steel plate door. And his own fear. His fear was the greatest barrier.

We cannot live without barriers, he thought, half-heartedly searching for poetry. *When the barriers are too few, we create our own.* He couldn't continue.

Nine double bunks were arranged in two semicircles at one end. Five in the outer loop and four inside. At the other end were four toilets surrounded by low walls that provided no privacy. And two showers. In between were two metal tables with attached bench. Enough to seat five. Eating was done in shifts. The room measured 24-feet by 24-four feet. Exactly. Jacob knew that because he had stepped it off again and again until his pacing seemed to make the other inmates nervous. No one asked him to stop, but he could see it in their eyes. So he climbed up to his bunk and sat with his legs dangling over the edge.

His neck and shoulders were sore from trying to brace himself with his hands laced behind his back as the pickup truck bounced and jolted over the washboard surface and the dips and bumps in the gravel road. Without a seat belt, he had been pummeled by the steel walls and unpadded benches. His glasses had been jarred off his face and he had been helpless to retrieve them as they bounced and ricocheted around the foot well. There was no air conditioning in the back, and his clothes were soaked with sweat by the time they pulled him from his cage at the field office north of Sells.

Agent Moody retrieved his glasses. One lens was pitted and the other cracked in the corner. "I'm sorry," she said as she gently slipped them over his nose. They hung there bent and askew. "You can make a claim for a new pair."

Then she had turned him over to the local sheriff's deputies, who snipped off his zip ties and replaced them with metal bracelets, which were attached in front to a belly chain. Jacob had to bend his neck to punch his glasses back onto his nose. They led him to an old gray Santa Cruz Sheriff's Department school bus. It was a worn and weathered antique with steel mesh welded over the windows. Waiting inside were half a dozen other sullen detainees, already on board. They were all seated apart from each other, and no one bothered to speak to him. The driver and a guard barked orders and seemed to be in a great hurry to be rid of them all. At least the seat was cushioned and there was a hint of cool air through the grillwork separating him from the front of the bus.

In Nogales deputies removed his handcuffs and belly chain and replaced them with an identical set. The old set apparently stayed with the bus. Paperwork seemed to change hands beyond his horizon, but no copies were given to him. They locked him into a small holding cell with a seatless metal toilet in one corner. There he waited for a long time.

"Don't I get a phone call?" he asked a deputy who passed his cell, but the man warned him to keep his mouth shut. He didn't ask again.

The sun was already setting when the van from Safford arrived. Again they changed his handcuffs and belly chain before ushering him into the back. There were no door handles on the inside. He was the only prisoner. A plate aluminum wall separated him from the deputies up front. Wire mesh covered the windows. For hours he felt utterly alone as they drove through the darkening desert.

In Safford the van pulled into the yard of the Graham County Sheriff's Adult Detention Center. Through spirals of concertina wire atop the chain link fence, Jacob had read the lofty words painted in grand gold letters high on the wall. He had never actually seen the inside of a jail, and the highfalutin language gave him hope that the facility would be better than what he routinely saw on television cop dramas. But the reality turned out to be much worse.

Inside two jailors, one young with buzz-cut strawberry blond hair, and the other white-haired and elderly, had removed the handcuffs and chains and relieved him of his wallet and cell phone and the other possessions in his pockets. He was ordered to take off his shoes, and they stripped him of his clothing. They handed him an orange jumpsuit and slippers to put on. The suit was too tight around the chest. They tried several sizes, but none fit right. Finally they settled on an extra large to accommodate his girth, but he had to roll up his sleeves and cuffs. The younger man grinned. "Makes ya look like a clown." Then they had him sign a receipt for his things, rolled his finger prints, and photographed him.

"You ain't eaten dinner yet?" the older deputy asked.

"No, sir."

"How long you been in custody?"

Jacob calculated. "Maybe about twelve hours."

"Shit. You gotta be fed."

"That's okay. I'm not hungry."

"Don't matter. It's the law. I'll have some dinner sent over to your cell."

The young deputy had handed him a thin mattress pad, a towel, a threadbare cotton blanket, and the stub of a toothbrush. Together they lead him down a long cement block hallway and unlocked a steel door. Jacob stepped inside and the jailors closed and locked the door behind him. A television blared out the voices and canned laughter of an inane sitcom. The inmates turned to eye him, but quickly lost interest. Jacob was just another worthless sad-sack clown who had strayed into the spider web. He wandered around aimlessly with his mattress and towel and blanket until one of the Caucasians, an emaciated druggie he later learned was called "Hump," jabbed his thumb at an upper bunk and snapped, "That's yours up there."

Jacob spread out his mattress and climbed up. Trying to avoid eye contact. Trying to be even more invisible than he already was. One glance told him that these fellows were not the sort of folks he was accustomed to associating with. They scared him. Even their disinterest scared him. *Especially* their disinterest scared him.

Jacob drew a deep breath and thought about what he had said to Agent Moody. *Don't let them train away your humanity.*

Five minutes later the lock snapped and a trustee in a gray jumpsuit pushed his way in with a tin plate in his hand. "Ramirez?" he barked.

After a pause, Jacob said meekly, "Here."

All eyes turned to him, as if he were a lone sheep in a pack of wolves. As if he were disturbing the order of the place.

"Your dinner," The trustee announced, rattling the plate on the nearest metal table and retreating. The lock clacked after him.

Jacob climbed down and stepped over to inspect a viscous pile of something green and black with tan specks in it. His stomach clinched at the aroma. What was it? Maybe it had some green beans mashed up in it. Some rice. Maybe some kind of ground meat, god knew what. A spoon and a slice of moldy bread lay next to it. His appetite evaporated.

"Yo."

Jacob turned around and met a slight, jittery young Apache fellow who looked too young to be in the adult lockup. He was not much older than a boy, with thick black hair trimmed short and a stubby chin that gave his head a squashed look.

"Ya gonna eat that?"

"No," he said. "Doesn't look fit for human consumption."

"Tha's a fac'." A quick smile flicked across the youth's narrow lips, revealing a gold front tooth. "Can I have it?"

"Yes. Sure. Go ahead."

Instead of eating it, the fellow scraped the plate into a couple of blank sheets of cheap writing paper and folded them up.

Jacob asked, "That for later?"

"Not for me." The gold tooth flashed again. "Summa these boys gets hungry later on. It be nice t' be able t' help 'em out when I can."

"What's you name?" Jacob asked.

"Grijavla," the young man announced proudly. He smiled broadly, his gold tooth glistening in the fluorescent lighting.

Jacob couldn't tell if it was his given or family name. Or an alias. It didn't matter. But he liked him. "I'm Jacob." He held out his fist.

Grijavla bumped it, clearly pleased to have made a new friend. "Wha'cha in for?"

Jacob frowned. "I'm not sure. I was picked up by the Border Patrol. But I was bussed up here by the sheriff's department. Nobody ever told me what I was charged with."

Grijavla scowled. "Thass bad, bro."

"Bad? How is it bad? I never crossed the border. It was all a mistake."

Grijavla laughed. "It's *all* a mistake, bro. That for sure. Yeah?

We don' get many border crossers up here. How come they sent ya up here, anyhow?"

Jacob just shrugged.

"I think they fuckin' with ya, man."

Jacob's spirits sank. "Why would they want to do that?"

Grijavla shook his head, then came the gold-studded grin. "'Cause they *can*. They *can*, bro. They the *man*."

Jacob spent the rest of the evening on his bunk, dangling his legs and punching his twisted glasses back on his nose. At ten o'clock the lights went out, but Jacob couldn't sleep. The time passed glacially. He lay still, forcing himself not to dwell on what had happened today. Or where this was all going.

Instead, the image of his brother filled him with waves of guilt and remorse. Alone in his bedroom at the back of the old house, Franklin lay dying. Jacob saw the room in all its detail. He envisioned the homestead that his father and his brother and he had scratched out of the harsh alkaline desert. The irrigation ditches. The planting and tending of corn and beans and squash and tomatoes. The booming monsoon rains. The smell of the greasewood afterward. And the wonderful adventures he and Franklin had had there together, exploring, fishing the ponds, laughing, imbibing their heritage infused on the dry desert air.

The guilty truth was that Jacob had not been a good brother. Oh, he had sent money. But not enough. Never nearly enough. It was all so clear now. Since he left for the university, he had not been back to help his brother with the work, because Jacob had grown enthralled with the possibility of fame and fortune in a foreign land.

3

By morning the cell had grown cold. Daylight filtered in from four round ports in the ceiling, one in each corner, too small to crawl through. Otherwise there was no way to tell if it was day or night. The steel door opened with a clang. A trustee rolled in a cart and began setting out mops and scrub brushes and rags. Everyone folded their mattresses and carried them over and stacked them on the empty cart. It all seemed to follow rules that everyone knew, but no one had bothered sharing with him.

Jacob jumped down, folded his mattress, and placed it on top of the stack as the trustee was wheeling out the cart.

Grijavla intercepted him on his way back to his bunk. He carried two mops and a bucket of sudsy water. "Gotcha on mop duty, ya lucky dog."

"We have to swab the floor?"

"Better'n scrubbin' the toilets, dawg."

"How did you manage that?"

"I jus' a'ksed Brodie, an' Jefe heard me an' nodded."

Jacob understood none of it, except there was a hierarchy here. And rules that these men had created, or perhaps those who had passed through before them. Rules which ordered life and made it endurable. He took hold of a mop, and for the first time felt an inkling of community here.

Grijavla prattled while they mopped. He was serving thirty days for being drunk in public. He had pled guilty. It was his third time, and next time he might qualify as a trustee. He lived over on the San Carlos reservation with his mother. The bottle was his curse.

When they were through and the equipment had been returned and counted and wheeled away, Jacob asked Grijavla what came next.

"Breakfast."

Jacob punched his broken glasses up on his nose. "How does that work?"

"You gonna eat last, bro. You at the bottom. Don't go pushin' yer way in. Wait'll there's an empty seat at the table."

"Okay."

"An' if ya can't finish your food, I wouldn't min' takin' your leftovers."

Jacob couldn't eat. The gruel they called oatmeal was lukewarm and vile. The toast was burnt. The last apple, passed over by every other inmate, was bruised and encrusted with scale. He left it all for Grijavla, who flashed a gleaming tooth in thanks.

After breakfast Grijavla sat next to him on the low tile wall by the toilets. They watched Scruggs, a wiry Latino from Douglas, collect all the Bibles that had been strategically placed throughout the cell. Scruggs tied them up in his blanket and began lifting and swinging them around as if he were pumping iron.

"Why all the Bibles?" Jacob asked.

"Baptists," Grijavla shrugged. "Mormons couldn't get their own Book in here." Then he nodded toward a stocky Mexican with a thick tattooed neck and shaved head who had turned to look the other way. "That's Jefe," he whispered. "Don' mess with him." He explained that Jefe was half-way through a year's sentence for beating his brother nearly to death. He was *numero uno* in here, and even the guards feared him. No one talked directly to him, except Brodie and Knife.

Jacob asked about the other inmates.

Most were in for driving violations, his friend told him. Drunk driving. Driving on a suspended license. Lee, a burly, hairy man, had beaten his wife and was now facing domestic abuse charges. It was unlikely they would stick, because his wife would never testify against him. If she did, she was as good as dead, and she knew it. Some were awaiting a disposition hearing or trial. Some were already serving time. Usually thirty days. Sometimes as much as six months. A few were waiting to be arraigned.

"Arraigned?" Jacob asked. "Will I be arraigned?"

"They gotta arraign ya, bro. Least I think they do. Don't know much about this federal shit, though."

"What do they do?"

"They jus' tell ya what they chargin' ya with. It's the law. Gotta do it within twenty-four hours, I think. They'll prob'ly call ya out this mornin'."

"I'll go up to court?"

"Naw. They do it on a video link. Just down the hall. Judge Claridge'll talk ta ya."

"Then what happens?"

"Usually they set bail. Or a disposition hearing. But I don't know nothin' 'bout how they do it with fed'ral pris'ners."

Mostly it was waiting. Jacob lay on his towel in his cold metal bunk. The radio pounded out tinny rock music at a deafening volume. Everyone seemed to keep their distance. Their own thoughts. Their own counsel. Four times a deputy clanged open the door and called out a name. The named inmate would follow the deputy out and return in five or ten minutes. Finally the deputy called out, "Ramirez!"

Jacob dropped to the floor and followed him down the cement block corridor to a small converted cell with a desk holding a video monitor with a face on it. The guard motioned him to the chair in front of it, and Jacob sat down.

"Good morning," said the face. It was a handsome young man with a full head of thick chestnut hair combed straight back. He wore a string tie, but no coat or robe. "I'm Wendell Claridge, Justice of the Peace. Can you hear me alright?"

"Yes," said Jacob.

"Good. What is your name?"

Jacob stated his name.

"It looks like they've got you on a federal hold, Mr. Ramirez." He appeared to turn pages below the screen. Jacob presumed it was his file. "But I can't find any charges filed." Claridge looked up. His eyes suggested intelligence. "What were you arrested for?"

"I don't know."

"They didn't tell you?"

"No. For being an Indian, I think."

Claridge smiled. "Tell me what happened."

Jacob told him everything. How his brother was dying of cancer. How Jacob had taken the old path home, but found it blocked. How he had crossed the first barrier, but had not reached the border fence. He described the confrontation with the Border Patrol agents and his arrest and his convoluted transportation to the jail.

"And no one advised you what you were being detained for?"

"That's correct, sir."

"Are you a United States citizen?"

"Yes, sir."

Claridge glanced down and nodded. "Yes, I see you have an Arizona driver's license." He paused in thought. "Do you remember who the arresting agent was?"

"His name tag said Nomellini, sir," Jacob answered.

"Uh," Claridge grimaced. "Okay. I wish he wouldn't keep doing this." He sighed. "I'll look into it. And put you on for a plea and disposition hearing tomorrow morning."

"*Tomorrow?*" Jacob punched his glasses back on his nose. "I'll have to stay in here another day?"

"It's all I can do."

"No bail?"

"Not with this federal hold."

"But my brother is dying. I should be there with him."

Claridge drew a deep breath and slowly exhaled. "I know. I'm sorry. But today my hands are tied."

Jacob couldn't remember walking back to the cell. Or climbing up to his bunk to dangle his legs into the void.

"Ya gotta pull yourself together, bro," Grijavla told him after Jacob explained what happened. "You be outta her tomorrow, for sure."

But Jacob wasn't sure about it at all. The hours dwindled by in a slow-motion dream. Depressed, he ate nothing for lunch, and Grijavla folded away his food. A couple of Grijavla's friends drifted over and bumped fists trying to cheer him up, but there was really not much to say. "Where're ya from?" "Whacha in for?" "Know a good cheap attorney?" Jacob didn't feel like talking. Instead he sat on his towel and let his feet dangle.

Dinner was inedible. Jacob had no appetite. Grijavla folded that away too. When the cart with the mattresses returned, he took one and lay quietly on it until the lights were turned out, and then the memories returned to engulf him. He didn't sleep for a long time.

4

The next morning they called his name shortly after breakfast. "Justice Claridge wants to see you up in the courtroom." In booking they reattached the handcuffs and belly chain before driving him over to the basement of the courthouse. They lead him up a narrow flight of metal stairs and through a steel door into the courtroom. A uniformed bailiff met them there and said, "You can take off the restraints, Hal. Judge says we don't need them."

Jacob gazed around the otherwise empty courtroom as the deputy found the right key and removed the cuffs and chain. At one end of the room stood the bench, raised only slightly above a long desk with six chairs and microphones. At the other end, behind a railing, were a dozen or so folding chairs and the main doorway.

"Justice Claridge will see you in chambers," the bailiff said. He opened a door at the side of the bench, but stayed outside as Jacob entered.

Claridge rose from the desk and offered Jacob his hand. "Please sit down, Mr. Ramirez."

Jacob sat opposite the judge.

"I talked to one of the agents who detained you."

"Nomellini?"

"No, the other agent."

"Moody," Jacob said, punching his glasses back on his nose.

"Yes. Very observant of you."

"I liked her."

"Yes, well . . . she liked you too . . . anyway, she looked you up on the internet. She's cancelled the federal hold. There are no other charges pending. Your record is clean. So I am ordering your release. Effective immediately."

Jacob stared at him. "I'm free to go?"

"Yes." Claridge smiled.

"That's it then?"

"Yes . . . after you've been processed out by the jail."

Jacob was a little confused, but elated. He started to his feet.

Claridge held up his hand. "There *is* one other thing."

"Oh?" Jacob sank back onto the chair, waiting for the other shoe to drop.

"Yes . . . ah . . . can you keep a secret, Mr. Ramirez?"

"A secret?"

"Yes." Claridge lowered his voice. "Agent Moody wanted you to know something. I ordinarily wouldn't be telling you this, but she specifically authorized me to. Now that the investigation is complete."

"Investigation?"

"This information cannot leave this room. Do I have your word?"

Jacob considered the ramifications. But he had no idea what Claridge was talking about. His curiosity got the better of him. "Yes, sir. You have my word."

"Agent Moody is not a trainee."

"She's not?"

"No. She's been with a special unit of the Border Patrol for over ten years, and when you met her she was working an undercover assignment for internal investigations." He paused to let it sink in. "There have been complaints."

"About . . . Nomellini?"

"Yes. And she thinks she's got him now for falsifying reports and unprofessional conduct toward detainees."

"But . . . *she* was writing the report, not Nomellini."

"He had to sign off on it. And he did."

"Well, won't that just be her word against his?"

Claridge leaned forward and whispered, "She was wearing a wire. It's all recorded."

Jacob's pout curled into a round smile.

"Looks like Nomellini's days as a field agent are over. He'll probably be retired."

Jacob just sat there smiling.

"It was important to Agent Moody that you be told all this. She also wanted to apologize for the grief you've been caused by this investigation. She wanted you to know that you will have played a big part in removing this bad apple from their ranks."

Jacob's head swam in a sea of conflicting emotion. Relief. Pride. Anger. Satisfaction. Slowly he rose to his feet.

"By the way," Claridge smiled, "she also told me she bought one of your books online." He held out his hand. "Now you get out of here and look after that brother of yours."

At the jail they returned his property. Jacob pulled on his clothes. Laced his shoes. Received his driver's license and wallet. No cash missing. His backpack. His cell phone. While he waited for the jailer to prepare the receipt, Jacob flipped open the phone. There was one voice message. He punched in the code and waited.

"Sign here," the deputy said.

Jacob signed the receipt.

The message was from his cousin Carlita in Mexico. Franklin died last night.

Jacob was utterly empty. Empty of purpose. Empty of direction. Empty even of the righteous anger he should have felt. His trip had been in vain. There was nothing left to be done.

The old jailor unlocked the steel door and pulled it open. The last barrier.

Jacob didn't move.

"You alright, son?" the jailor asked. "Ya look a little shaky."

"My brother died."

It took a moment for the words to register. "While you was in *here*?"

"Yes, sir."

"I'm so sorry."

Jacob could see that he really was. He nodded his appreciation, and had to punch his glasses back onto his nose. But still he didn't move. Franklin was gone. There was nothing for him out there.

The jailor stepped away. "Take your time, son. I'll keep an eye on ya from the cage and be back to close the door."

The door stood wide open before him.

Jacob understood at last. *A barrier is only a barrier if I am trying to cross to the other side. There are no barriers, except the ones I create in my mind. And if there are no longer barriers in my mind . . . then there are no barriers at all.*

Slowly he stepped out into the blinding sunlight.

Three New Years

It was almost midnight, and Evan Layton knew he would ring in the new year on a cold taxiway of the Indianapolis International Airport. Boarding had been delayed nearly two hours, and for another hour he had been strapped into the motionless dim tube of an aircraft, with the engines vibrating and the air vents whooshing. Thick snowflakes were beginning to fall outside the window as midnight approached.

Ding! went the intercom.

"This is the captain." The voice was infused with a slow, confident Texas drawl. "I want to apologize for the delay. The weather in Chicago seems to be getting worse, rather than better, and we still do not have clearance for takeoff. If we can't get out within the next fifteen minutes, we're going to have to return to the gate." Pause. "We now have about . . . five minutes left in 2018. Complimentary champagne is on board, but the flight attendants won't be able to serve it until after we're airborne. I'll be back to count down to the New Year with you."

Evan resettled his buttocks and arched his back. He wanted to stand, but the seat belt light remained on. Thank God he had upgraded to first class. Here the seats were wider and there was more leg room and fewer passengers. He had spent a chunk of his frequent-flier miles for the upgrade, but, hell, he wasn't going to be using them anyway. Not where he was going . . .

Ding!

The captain came on again. "Thirty seconds to the New Year . . . now twenty . . . ten . . . five, four, three, two, one. Happy New Year y'all! Happy 2019!"

Evan heard a couple of cheers and a horn toot from behind the steerage class curtain. But not in the first class cabin. There would be no celebration here. It was almost empty. Three rows, four seats each, total of twelve, with only three occupants. Across the aisle a heavy-set, dowdy woman in a plaid woolen suit ignored him, her window shade drawn down and her eyes closed. Two rows ahead of her an elderly fellow, whose silver stands spilled over the seatback, made no sign of having even heard.

Ding!

"I have some good news for y'all." Having paused to let the excitement pass, the captain continued in his comforting drawl, "There seems to be a hole in the overcast and we've got some movement up at the head of our queue, so we might just get out of here tonight. I'll keep you updated."

Evan settled back into his musings. No, he wouldn't be needing his frequent flier miles where he was going. He was bound for San Francisco to be sentenced. On Monday morning a federal judge would decree his sentence for corporate securities fraud and insider trading. There had been no trial. He had pleaded guilty. The evidence against him was overwhelming once his former friend and colleague Angelo Chiric had turned state's evidence. Evan's plea was in exchange for dismissal of a racketeering charge, the possibility of a lighter sentence, and for his agreement to cooperate with the FBI. Still, he was facing a maximum of twenty years in a federal penitentiary and an unsympathetic judge.

Ding!

"This is the captain again. Good news. We've been cleared to proceed to runway 23R to hold for takeoff. We're third in line. Once we're airborne it'll be a little bumpy until we reach cruising altitude, so I'm going to ask you to keep your seat belts fastened until I turn off the seatbelt light. Flight attendants, prepare for departure."

The whine of the engines ramped up and the jetliner began to roll through the now lightly-sticking snow. One after another the first two aircraft crawled into position and began their clumsy acceleration down the whitening runway. And then came his plane's slow pirouette into place and the hold before takeoff. The engines roared and the slow crawl picked up speed as Evan was pressed into the seat cushions. The gently falling snow flakes became horizontal blurs in the landing lights. It seemed forever to attain escape velocity. At last the wings flexed upward, the landing gear bumped a final bump, and they were soaring free of the ground. Evan watched the lights of the world fall away until everything outside was swallowed by the clouds.

Evan sank back into his seat. His thoughts were now of his mother. Her features were already beginning to fade and meld with those earlier memories of her. Never again would he see that face. Never. This trip had been to say goodbye forever. In her darkened livingroom, which still smelled of his childhood and had not changed since his father died, she had beseeched him to pray with her. She had lit a single candle, and before it they knelt together. She prayed out loud. To a God he did not believe in. She prayed for a miracle. Which he didn't believe in. She prayed for her son to be given a second chance. Which he knew was not going to happen.

He closed his eyes. His breathing slowed and deepened. He saw leaves spiraling down, one by one, like golden snowflakes, shaken loose from the autumnal crown above, trembling in the light breeze and leaving behind the barren branches forever. The leaves were stories. Each was a story. Stories told on the news about war and the weather and automatic rifle fire at a movie theater. Stories told by friends about themselves or about his hometown, now almost forgotten. But mostly they were the stories he told himself. Stories to construct a context in which to fit all the movement and the feeling and the planning and the remembering. Stories to create a meaning out of the chaos–"

Ding!

"This is the captain." It was the same slow, confident drawl. "A few minutes ago we crossed into the Central Time Zone. So you can set your clocks back one hour. We will be celebrating the New Year all over again in about . . . another twenty-five minutes. I'll give you the new count-down, and then we'll break out the champagne." Pause. "We're now cruising at thirty-nine thousand, and it should be smooth up here all the way until we begin our descent into San Francisco."

Those words sent a chill down Evan's spine.

"So I'm turning off the seatbelt sign, but please keep 'em fastened loosely while you're in your seats. Sit back and enjoy the flight."

"*Descent into San Francisco,*" Evan muttered to himself. The phrase seemed uncommonly apt. As in Dante's descent into hell. It would be a repeat of a similar descent three years ago. That flight had originated in New York, but the arrival timing was almost the same. The wee hours of New Year's morning. 2016.

Angelo had been waiting for him at the gate. Angelo Chiric and he were about his same age. Mid-thirties back then. Angelo was lean and hungry, always sharply dressed, with slicked-back black hair, an engaging smile, and a quick wit and tongue. They had been working together as investment brokers for almost a decade by then, growing up with the firm. Angelo had earned a higher position, due mostly to his suave rapport with the senior partners. But Evan brought home more money, because their compensation was based on commissions, and Evan was good at what he did. Good with the numbers. Good with the hunches.

Angelo had met him at the gate and led him out to the parking garage where they climbed into his new black BMW M8. As they cruised north on the Bayshore Freeway, Angelo excitedly introduced him to his devilishly simple foolproof get-rich-quick money laundering scheme. Evan couldn't believe what he was hearing. It all sounded crazy. And dangerous. But as they drove Angelo had talked and wheedled and Evan began to . . .

He unsnapped his seatbelt and clawed his way into the aisle, where he stood, head swimming. Evan didn't want to think about Angelo anymore. He should never have listened to that fucking Judas to begin with. And now it was all too late anyway. He found his way into the lavatory and peed and splashed cold water on his face. His eyes were bloodshot, and he felt weary to the bone. He didn't want to think about any of it anymore. He wanted to sleep.

Back in his seat Evan reclined and closed his eyes. Blood rushed in his ears above the drone of the aircraft engines. He began to doze.

Ding!

"Uh," Evan groaned, for a moment unsure where he was. Or *when* he was.

"This is the captain," spoke a clipped and precise voice. Almost British. "For those of you who want to try ringing in the New Year again, you have about thirty seconds to prepare . . . twenty . . . ten . . . five, four, three two, one, Happy New Year! Again. Happy 2018!"

"Nineteen," Evan corrected. "It's 2019."

"The flight attendants will be bringing around a complimentary glass of champagne and free snacks and beverages. Meals and alcoholic beverages will be available for those of you who wish to purchase them."

Evan wondered what had happened to the pilot with the Texas drawl? He shrugged it away. The cockpit must hold more than one pilot.

After a while a weary, middle-aged woman in a flight attendant outfit brought champagne from a rolling cart. She served a couple of passengers two rows ahead whom Evan hadn't noticed before. The woman across the aisle was gone. Probably to the lavatory. He couldn't see the silver-haired fellow up front. He was probably lying down asleep. Evan accepted a plastic glass of champagne and a "Happy New Year," but declined anything more than a couple of bags of mixed nuts to munch on. His stomach was far too knotted to try a meal. He stuffed his cup with the empty nut bag wrappers and set it on the seatback tray. He leaned his chair back. He dozed.

Ding!

Evan came awake with a paralyzing chill of terror gnawing at his insides. His limbs felt numb. For an instant the menace was inchoate. Unfinished. Deep and piercing. Something very bad was going to happen.

"This is the Captain speaking. We are now in the Mountain Time Zone. You can set your clocks back another hour."

Slowly, as the British voice spoke, Evan began to recognize the fear he had lived with for so long after the shit hit the fan. The chill of certain doom, coupled with an insipid hope that he could yet avoid the consequences of his deeds.

"I'll count down to New Years for you shortly."

Evan was reliving the terror of the early days of the investigation. His heart palpitated. A cold sweat dampened his shirt. Before him stood the FBI agent . . . Farley was his name . . . who was trying to persuade him to turn state's evidence against Angelo to save his own skin. "Mr. Chiric is considering turning on you," Farley said. "You'd better beat him to the punch. It'll save you a lot of grief later down the road. You'll get a better deal than he will. Serve a lot less time, if any at all. You're going down anyway, one way or the other. Both of you."

But Evan stood his ground. He trusted Angelo. They were like brothers. He knew Angelo would never turn on him. But still . . .

"Can I take your cup?"

Evan jerked. The attendant had sneaked up from behind. He

dumped the cup into the plastic sack she was offering.

"Can I get you anything else?"

He shook his head dumbly. He felt like he had fallen through a crack between worlds, and didn't trust himself to speak. Afterward, he drifted quietly in his seat, trying to nap, trying not to think.

Ding!

"We're going to have another opportunity to ring in the New Year in about a minute." The voice was female. All business, but definitely a female purr. Evan wondered how many pilots were up there. "This will be your third time on this flight, and you may be getting a little tired of it. But here we go anyway . . . twenty . . . ten, nine, eight, seven, six, five, four, three two, one, Happy New Year! For the third time. Happy 2017!"

"Is this some kind of a joke?" Evan asked no one, because the first class cabin appeared to be empty. "It's 2019. You don't lose a whole fucking year every time you cross a time zone. Just an hour."

He drew a deep breath, trying to settle his nerves. And then another. Something was happening to him he couldn't understand. It was probably just a panic attack, like he used to get as a kid. The solution was always to breathe deeply. Quiet meditation. Calm. Let them play their little jokes. It was nothing to him. But why did she say 2017? That was the year things began to go wrong. That's why their little joke upset him so. He tried to put it all out of his mind. He tried to sleep.

Ding!

"We are just crossing into California and the Pacific Time Zone." The voice approximated the southern drawl of the original pilot, but maybe not quite so Texas. "You can all set your clocks back another hour. Which tucks us back into the old year again. We've already been assigned a gate and it looks like we'll be arriving in San Francisco about half past midnight on New Year's morning. Maybe a little bit sooner, depending on traffic. I'll let you know when it's time to celebrate the New Year for the final time on this flight. Looks like about 20 minutes to go now."

Evan closed his eyes. A golden leaf fluttered past in the sunlight. After a while, so did another. They were so few now. They were the stories he told himself. He could feel them slipping from his memory.

The skeletal winter branches were almost bare. With each leaf he felt a pang of regret. And the calm of release.

Ding!

"The weather in San Francisco is clear with calm winds and a temperature of 48 degrees. You've got a little over a minute before celebrating the New Year again. I'll count down then."

Ding!

"Okay, fifteen seconds . . . ten . . . five, four, three, two, one, Happy New Year!"

Evan watched the lights of the Bay Area drift into view. The black water had bitten big chunks out of them. As the plane descended and banked north, the individual buildings and streets and cars became discernable. Then came the rumble of the landing gear and the rush over the rippled water and the thunk of the touchdown and the roar of the reverse thrusters braking.

Evan was the first to deplane. With his carry-on bag slung over one shoulder, he trundled alone up the steep jet ramp toward the bright lights of the concourse ahead. It felt like climbing out of a tunnel from an earthen burrow into daylight. Strange things had gone on in that aircraft, but he could no longer remember precisely what they were. A nightmare was fading and forgotten in the light of dawn, leaving behind only an ambiance of dread and doom.

Angelo emerged from the crowd, black hair slicked back and grinning. "Happy New Year, man!" He clasped Evan in a big California bear hug and pounded him on the back. When Evan's response was less than vigorous, he pulled back. "You look a little frazzled, man. Something happen in New York?"

"What year is this?"

"Boy, what've you been drinking on that plane? It's 2016. The New Year has arrived."

The answer seemed somehow *wrong* to Evan, but he couldn't quite put his finger on the problem. "Weird," he said out loud.

"What's weird, man?"

"2016."

Angelo considered for a moment, then laughed. "Yeah. Okay. I see what you're gettin' at. How'd we ever live this fucking long?

Astonishes me too. What with all the drinking and partying and the drugs."

That wasn't what Evan meant. He didn't really know what he had meant. He shifted his feet. "Well, anyway, thanks for picking me up. I hope I'm not interrupting a hot date or anything."

"No," Angelo grinned, threading his way down the thinly populated concourse. "Tonight, they're *all* hot, and we still got time to make some moves."

Evan shook his head. "I think I'm too beat. I already celebrated the fucking New Year four times on the plane." He described the runway delay and passing through four time zones. "It just sorta sapped everything outta me."

"That's good, in a way," Angelo told him seriously. "I got something I wanna talk to you about anyway. Something really big. After we get in the car."

A powerful feeling of deja vu washed over Evan. Intertwined with it was an ineffable terror of great moral hazard. But he said nothing, and the feeling subsided as they wound their way in silence out into the parking garage.

"Voila!" Angelo bowed and swept out his arm like a matador as he pushed the unlock button on his fob. A black BMW flashed its lights in response.

"Whoa. That's your car?"

"Damn right! A brand new M8. I just picked it up today. Or I guess it was yesterday now. Can't really afford it, but that's why I wanted to run something by you." He pulled open the passenger door. "Climb on in."

Angelo explained the scam as they drove. At first Evan couldn't believe what he was hearing. But the last disorienting vapors of that fading deja vu kept him silent. Angelo held out a large brown clasp envelope. "Don't let anybody else see this. If it falls into the wrong hands, we're probably both fucked. Burn the contents when you're done with 'em."

"What is it?"

"Some preliminary calculations I've done. It all looks watertight and safe to me. I've gone over them a million times. It all looks safe.

But you're the whiz at numbers, and I want you to work them through yourself. To make sure we don't get ourselves into a real mess."

Evan reluctantly accepted the envelope. He did not open it. He had a bad feeling about the whole thing.

Angelo dropped him off at his rented cottage in Menlo Park. "Get back to me on this as soon as you can, okay? Maybe tomorrow?"

"I'll see."

Evan went inside and built a small fire in the hearth. He felt chilled to the bone. It was more than the draftiness of the empty room or his lack of sleep. There was something morally chilling about the moment. Before the blazing fire he rocked from foot to foot, trying to remember something elusive that faded further away as he tried to grasp it. And then it was gone. He shifted from stocking foot to stocking foot as he transferred the envelope back and forth from hand to hand.

One part of him wanted to open it and see what Angelo was so excited about. What could it hurt? Evan was curious. Curious to see if he would be able to spot the flaws.

But another part knew he should just toss the damned thing unopened into the blaze and be done with it.

Foot to foot, hand to hand, Evan wavered before the flickering fires of hell.

It was time to decide.

Pardners

1

"Hey, stranger . . . y'look kinda lost. Kin I buy y'a drink?"

The friendly cowboy sat alone at the bar, the heels of his boots hooked into the middle strut of the tall wooden stool where he perched, because his legs were too short to reach the brass rail. His face was round and chubby in the shadow of his wide-brimmed, high-domed Stetson hat. His denim trousers were patched and worn, but clean. A fine leather vest was wrapped over a light blue cotton work shirt, frayed at the elbows. He bore neither sidearm nor spurs.

The lithe, rangy fellow in the charcoal three-piece suit squinted through the barroom gloom to inspect the shorter man. Then he smiled. "Don't mind if I do," he replied, tipping his hat and easing himself onto the adjacent barstool.

"Ain't seen you around here a'fore," the cowboy said. His eyes were rheumy and his breath ripe with sour whiskey from having gotten a good early start on his morning tipple. His face was tanned and deeply creased from age and too many years of too much sun. A long moustache, streaked with gray, turned down at the corners of his mouth, presenting a seriousness of mood that belied his congeniality. "Where y'from?"

"East," the stranger said. "Bound west."

"With the railroad?"

The stranger paused a beat, then said, "That I am. You've got a good eye."

"Don't look like no track layer t'me. You must work the combines, huh?"

"No. I'm a lawyer."

"Well . . . *I'll be damned!* Ain't never bought a drink for no railroad *lawyer* before. *Javier!*" He raised his hand and caught the attention of the swarthy Mexican washing glasses in a bucket. "I'm Willie Crandyke. What're ya havin' Mister . . . ?"

"Gunnerson." The man held out a dexterous hand. "Lucas Gunnerson at your service."

Willie Crandyke shook Gunnerson's firm grip, which was rougher and more callused than he had expected from a lawyer. "Glad t'meet'cha."

When the stocky young bartender finally made his way over, Gunnerson asked him, "Got any beer?"

"*Lo siento*, all out today, *senior*."

"Whiskey?"

"*Hay*. I have plenty whiskey."

"I'll have a whiskey, then. My friend here said he's buyin'–"

"*Dios, Willy!* You overdrawn *ya*!"

"Just until payday, Javier. You know I'm good for it."

The lawyer held up a quick hand. "Hold on. I'm buyin' this round. For both me and Willy here." He dug a gold coin out of the watch pocket of his vest and slapped it on the bar. "Got something to celebrate today anyway."

"What you celebrating, *senior*?" asked Javier as he pulled up an extra shot glass and wiped it out with a dirty bar rag. He poured it and Willy's full to the lip.

"Yeah, what's yer good news?" Willy chimed in.

"Gentlemen, I'm sorry . . . but it's a private matter. Cheers." He hoisted his shot glass, sipped the sharp raw liquor, and set it back down on the bar nearly full.

Down the saloon a big, sweaty cowpuncher wiped his face with a red bandana and hollered out for more whiskey. Javier left to tend him.

Willy tossed back his shot and smacked his lips. "You got a secret, eh?" He leaned in and whiskey fumes engulfed them both. "Well, I'll tell y'somethin'. I got me a pretty good damn' secret m'self."

"That's a fine thing. Having a secret makes life interesting. And keeps a man going sometimes. Until the time comes to share our secrets. What do you do for a living, Willie?"

"Me? Oh . . . well, I'm a stagecoach driver. Or used t'be, anyhow. I still get a call now an' then t'fill in at Kinnear. Mostly when young

Harlan Evers or Percy Jones or one o' the other drivers gets 'emselves hurt an' can't make a haul." He puffed up his chest. "But I used t'be pretty good."

"Pretty good, huh?"

"Yup. Use t'be one o'the best reinsmen in these parts."

The lawyer took another toxic sip from the shot glass while Willy eyed him, puckering and wondering when they might get on to the next round.

"Use to," the lawyer reflected. "Must've been an interesting line of work. You must've seen yours share of outlaws."

"That I did. That I did. Outlaws and *banditos* and *pistoleros*. Even a renegade Injun'r two, back when I first started hauling the mail wagon for Butterfield and then the big coaches up through Dos Cabezas and Apache Pass. I sure seen my share. I even had one day when Mexicans and outlaws and Injuns all three came after the stage."

"All three in one day?"

"Yessir. But I always managed t'keep myself from gettin' kilt." He eyed Gunnerson's glass. "Say, that there ain't sippin' whiskey, y'know. That whiskey's for tossin' back and swallowin' down hard before your throat grips up."

Gunnerson laughed. "You sure it won't make a person go blind."

Willy joined the fun. "Ain't yet . . . but I keep on a'tryin'."

"Here, Willy, why don't you finish mine. My taste is a little off today." Gunnerson slid his shot glass over the polished bar. "I don't imagine they run much through Apache pass any more."

"No sir. Not since the railroad come through Benson an' Willcox." He tossed back the whiskey and grimaced. "Thank ya." He belched. "Stage and wagon routes run mostly north an' south nowadays. Down t'Douglas an' Bisbee. Kinnear runs up t'Tucson. An'er's a new route up through the Gila valley t' Show Low. Not much work left in these parts. Sometimes I fill in down at the stable now. I'm good with animals."

"Tell me about your run-in with the Apaches and the bandits and the Mexicans all in one day, will you, Willy? Sound's pretty interesting."

"Well . . . it's a good long story . . . an' kind thirsty work . . ."

Gunnerson waved away the objections. "I've got the time. Let me get a bottle of something a little better quality and a couple of fresh glasses. Then why don't you and I go on over to that table in the back, where we'll be a little more comfortable and private. What do you say?"

"Pardner, you just bought yourself a yarn."

2

Well . . . let's see. This was a long time ago. Back in sixty. Or maybe sixty-one. I recall the days t'be short an' the nights was cold. Cold enough to bring along buffalo robes for the passengers. This was all still New Mexico Territory then. It all happened 'bout midday. We was haulin' a Concord with a team a' six draft horses outta Dragoon Springs and was a'headin' for Apache Pass. This was a'fore the war an' Butterfield hadn't yet shut down that route. Harlan Evers was drivin' and I was ridin' brake an' shotgun. *Old* Harlan, that was. Not his boy, who's got the same moniker. Young Harlan's still a driver for Kinnear. Old Harland, *this* was. He's now dead.

Anyhow . . . remember, this was twenty-five some years gone by . . . but I still remember some'a it like it happened jus' yesterday. We was pullin' up outta the playa and into the foothills with a light load. Four passengers, as I recall. Two nuns and a young man with his pretty little wife. There mighta been one or two more I can't recall. But none of 'em knew how to handle a shootin' iron. That was the main thing. An' probably a good thing, too, lookin' back. So it was all up to me and Harlan to see that we got them and the mail safe through to El Paso.

Well . . . as I was a'sayin' . . . we was a'climbin' up outta that alkali an' greasewood sink an' into the low mesquite an' yucca, an' I turned around and see these two Mexicans crossin' the playa behind us. They was ridin' fancy, good-lookin' horses, an' a'gainin' on us. My eyesight was pretty good back then, so I could make out all the copper and silver sparkling in the sun off'a their saddles an' those big fancy *tan galán* sombreros. And as they got nearer, I saw they were armed with pistols and rifles and bandoliers a'criss-crossin' their chests. These weren't no poor *campesinos* out havin' a little fun. No siree. These fellows looked t'me to be well-armed *banditos* on serious business. "Oh, oh," I says to Harlan. "We got trouble." Harlan cranks around an' takes a long look an' whips them horses into a faster trot. Not that we could outrun 'em.

But we figured we might just make it up to Dos Cabezas, though what good that mighta done us, I really don't know. They got no lawman there an' never did.

Now here's sump'in y'need'a keep in mind. We jus' so happened t'be carryin' a special mail satchel bound for Santa Fe, which was the territorial capital at the time. One of those fine scrolled-leather satchels with a wax seal. It was postmarked outta some Mexican gover'ment office down in Hermosillo. Never saw anything like that before. But I figured it must be important. And I figured it had somethin' t'do with them Mexican *caballeros* behind us, since we weren't carrying no cash or bullion or even a strongbox on this particular trip. I told Harlan what was on my mind. "Hide it," he told me, and that's jus' what I done. I found that Mexican satchel in one o'the mail bags tied to the rail on top and rolled it up into a old grease rag and stuck it down in the foot well under some spare tackle and put my footboard back on top. Y'see, I always needed my own special footboard, being so slight o' stature.

But the trail got windy and pretty soon I couldn't see 'em back there no more, which I considered good luck, but a bit odd. Lookin' back, I think they mighta spotted Injun lookouts up on the rim and decided t'pull back an' catch up with us later. Nothin' them renegade Injuns liked better'n killin' Mexicans.

Anyhow, just before town, the road veers into an arroyo with a lay o' sand that slows down the coach a might. No sooner were we into that soft sand than a cowboy with a bandana over his face rides out from behind one of those big, rocky cut banks and fires his six-shooter into the blue sky. Twice, as I recall. I grab for the shotgun, but three more masked bandits ride up alongside, two from my side an' one from Harlan's. So I let go o'the shotgun and Harlan and me put our hands up inta the air. Harlan and me had talked it over before a time'r two, an' mail pouches just ain't worth gettin' kilt for. I shouted down and tried to calm the passengers inside, but they was already in stone shock.

"Throw down that scattergun," the man in front hollers. He rode the biggest piebald stallion y' ever seen. I could a'sworn I'd seen that horse someplace before, but jus' couldn't recollect where. I did what he said, slow an' easy. Didn't want no misunderstanding, an' I didn't want t'ding up the barrel o' that nice ol' gun.

"Now throw down your gun belts."

Well, Harlan an' me both wore sidearms, but we didn't use 'em much. Neither of us could hit an adobe wall at ten paces. But the company issued 'em to us. Wanted us t'wear 'em to give comfort t'the passengers when we was haulin' through Injun country. We was glad to be rid of 'em.

"Now throw down them mail bags," he says.

I unhitch 'em, one after the other, eight of 'em in all, and drop 'em t'the ground. Two o'the men dismounted and untied the sacks and spilt 'em into the sand, then kicked through 'em with their boots, lookin' for somethin' in particular. Then they order the passengers out and began rooting around through the cabin and untie the boot in back an' dump all the luggage an' open everthing up an' spilt it all out into the sand. By then I had a pretty good notion what they was a'lookin' for.

"Get down!" the head *honcho* yells up at Harlan an' me.

Well, Harlan an' me we climbed down an' stood over by the passengers. The man's wife looked t'me like she was 'bout to faint in the hot sun. So with my hands still in the air I managed to shoo all the women and the husband feller over into the shade of some mesquite while the bandits threw everything out of the coach. Everything except my footboard and what lay beneath it.

Finally the leader walks over t'Harlan an' me and points his revolver right into our faces. First Harlan. Then me. Then Harlan again. That scared the Jesus outta me. An' that's when I think I recognized him. Up close like that. His reddish hair. The pie he's a'ridin'. The particular smell o' him. I figgered it was a man named "Dour" or me'be "Dire." A foreman from the McPhearson spread over by Whitewater Draw. "Where's the satchel?" he demands. Harlan and me both act innocent. Like we had no idea what he was talkin' about. But I think he knew better. An' I think he might've kilt us both right then and there if'n I hadn't told him where it was hid.

No sooner had one of his hands dug the satchel out from neath my footboard than the Apaches show up. It started with a rifle shot up the draw. Then another. Then some serious whoopin'. An' a half-dozen Chiricahua braves came a'ridin' down at us from up the arroyo. Dour and his boys jump inta their saddles and scramble off west down the trail with nary a concern 'bout what might befall us'n. They'd got what they came for.

Now, say what y'may about Apaches, but they got a certain amount of honor an' respect for ya if ya behave yerself like a man. Don't show'm no fear. An' that's jus' what Harlan and me tried t'do. The passengers huddled back around the stage lookin' more scared than little child'un. We let the Injuns look around through the spilt mail. Through all the stuff spilled outta those suitcases. They picked out a few little things. I recollect a little pearl hair comb, for one. A few other odds an' end not worth much. The mail didn't interest 'em. When they saw there weren't no strongbox an' nothing t'steal, they began pokin' over the horses.

Well, that's when Harlan has his bright idea. He jumps out yellin' this Injun gobbledygook I never heard before, the same thing over and over again, and pointin' and slapin' the necks of our two lead horses. Somewise he had learnt the Chiricahua word for "gift," an' he was offerin' them blood-thirsty rascals our two lead drays. Well, that seemed t'settle 'em down. Brightened 'em up a bit. One of 'em even smiled and nodded like he just got hisself a birthday present. We help 'em unharness those two small lead horses, an' off they set, happy as chil'en at Christmastime. An' we hung on t'our scalps.

When things settled down, I look Harlan in the eye an' said, "Whadda we do now?" With our two best lead horses gave away, we would never get that big stagecoach outta the sand an' up an' over Apache Pass. An' y'got t'remember that this was before Fort Bowie was put up there. Or any soldiers t'give us a hand. So we was on our own. A'course the safety of the passengers was our chief concern. That was the Butterfield code. Look after the passengers first and foremost. An' so far we had done jus' that. So, we reckoned the only thing left t' do was t'turn back to Dragoon Springs station and make a report.

It took some while t'get underway. The passengers shook out their clothes and folded 'em back into their suitcases and bags as best they could. Then they helped Harlan and me stuff the mail back into the mail sacks. Not in any particular order, but that was for the mail service to sort out later. They could just thank us for not losin' any of it. Then Harlan and me tied everything back on board and manage to turn the rig around, which was not so easy in that soft sand with a team of only four drays.

But we managed it.

Now, comin' down the highway we ran into them Mexicans *pistoleros* again. They hailed us to a stop, but nobody drew their guns. They left their rifles in their scabbards an' their pistols in their holsters. But I knew they's a lot faster'n us. They had that look o' real gunslingers. I just kept the shotgun across my lap, pointed sidewise at nothin' in particular, casual like, with one arm on it an' the other on the brake shaft. We all smiled a lot. How do y'do an' howdy well met. We told 'em what'd happened. They asked about the satchel. They knew about that all right. Harlan and me looked at each other and I told 'em the robbers had took it. An' nothin' else got took. They asked for a description of the robbers, an' I told 'em all I knew. So did Harlan. An' that seemed t'satisfy 'em jus' fine.

3

Willy's glass was still half-full, just the way Gunnerson had poured it nearly an hour before. Willy had been so taken up by his own story, that he'd forgotten to drink. The bottle sat between them almost full. Now he took a big swig from his glass and swallowed it slowly. "Y'know . . . an' I hate t'tarnish a good yarn . . . but, lookin' back, I sometimes get a notion that them Mexicans wasn't there t'steal that satchel from us at all. I reckon those fellas might'a been there t'see that it got through to Santa Fe." He took another sip, rolled the liquor on his tongue, and smacked his lips. "I could get used t'this stuff."

"Kentucky straight bourbon whiskey," Gunnerson replied. "Aged five years. I'm surprised they had any in stock."

"Oh, Tombstone ain't so backwards a place as y'may think. They even got an opry house here." He read the label on the bottle. "Must'a cost ya a pretty penny. I'm much obliged. You fellas must do perty good for yourselves lawyerin' for the railroad."

"We do alright," Gunnerson admitted, sipping from his own glass. Then he set it down decisively and looked the cowboy in the eye. "Willy . . . you know that big secret of yours you were telling me about. I think I got an idea what it might be."

Startled, Willy seemed to sober up.

"And I've got a proposition for you," Gunnerson continued affably. "I'll tell you my secret, if you tell me yours."

Willy glanced around the saloon, suddenly uncomfortable.

"If I can guess what yours is all about, that is," the lawyer hedged. "And your secret will be safe with me. Client confidentiality."

"What's 'at?"

"It just means as a lawyer, I'm bound never to divulge a word of what you tell me."

"Kinda like a priest, uh?"

"Yes. Kind of like your confessor. Probably do you some good to get that weight off your shoulders and share it with someone else. Bare your soul. Don't you think it's about time?"

Willy thought about it, but didn't answer. Finally he said, "Okay, mister know-all railroad lawyer, whadda ya think my little secret's all about."

Gunnerson leaned in. "That Mexican courier pouch with those papers, Willy. Where is it?"

Willy glanced away. He started to get up, then changed his mind and sank back down, thinking it through.

"I believe you know a fellow named Tillman?" Gunnerson asked. "Orin Tillman?"

Willy couldn't hide the shock in his eyes. He looked down at his boots. Fiddled with the brass buttons on his vest. "Lemme see. Tillman. Tillman. No. No, can't say that I ever heard o' no Orin Tillman. Why d'y'ask?"

"Because I took his deposition a couple of weeks back. Over in Yuma. At the Territorial prison. And he said you still have those Mexican documents."

"Well . . . he was a'lyin'."

Gunnerson watched the old stage driver, then he spoke softly. "That's just the thing, Willy. I don't believe that he was. You see, he was scheduled to be hung first thing the next morning. For some crimes that had nothing to do with you. All his ill deeds seemed to have caught up with him at once. The man had just spent more than an hour with a priest in his cell and tears were streaming down his cheeks. He was trying to make peace with his God. He spelled out the details of one or two other crimes involving young boys that the state had no idea he was even involved in. No, he wasn't into lying that afternoon. He was into telling the truth and getting it all off his chest and cleansing his soul. He was about to meet his Maker."

"You was there?"

"Oh yes, I was. On behalf of the railroad. Railroad's been looking for those Mexican land grant deeds for over twenty-five years. Orin Tillman was on the top of the list of suspects, so when they found him my supervisor sent me over to take his deposition. Thought he might lead us to them."

Willy looked up, interested. "Wha'd Tillman say."

"I asked him about that stagecoach robbery, the one you just told me about, and he freely admitted he was responsible for it. Told us pretty much the same story you did. He and the boys from the Lazy J who were with him. Just like you told it, but not exactly. Here's where the big difference lies: he said he and his boys never found those documents. They never found that hand-tooled leather courier pouch you were describing, either. He said you and Harlan never handed any of it over to him before the Apaches came. He suspected you still had them."

"He's a'lyin'," Willy repeated, but without much conviction.

"He swore to me on his immortal soul that he was telling the truth."

Both men fell silent. Willy had lost his appetite for hard spirits. He fiddled with his empty glass. After a while he looked up and asked in a meek voice, "If'n I had 'em . . . an' I ain't a'sayin' that I *do* have 'em, but *if'n* I did . . . would I be goin' t'jail?"

Gunnerson straightened up and smiled. "No, Willy. I give you my word on that. Statute of limitations has expired. I had a talk with this attorney I went to law school with . . . he's now a big time criminal attorney in Tucson and knows the U S Attorney and Prosecuting Attorney for the Arizona Territory . . . and he agreed with my arguments that locating and producing those documents were more important than putting a broken-down old stagecoach driver behind bars."

"Broke-down am I?" Willy grinned and then laughed out loud. "We'll see who's broke-down."

"So you'll help me out?"

"Doin' what?"

"Well . . . for starters . . . by telling me the truth."

Willy considered his options. "An' what's in it for me?"

"I can make it worth your while. I assure you that. But let's talk about it after I've had a chance to examine the condition of those deeds. For starters, I'll give you one-hundred dollars, cash, just to take a look."

Willy just sat there stunned, shaking his head. He stood slowly, like a man in a dream.

Gunnerson stood with him and took his arm. He understood the man's conflict. "Let's just go take a look at them, Willy. You have nothing to lose in doing that. And you may learn what they were all about. After all these years. And we can figure out what's the best thing for you to do after that. Either way, you keep the hundred dollars."

Willy wandered through the saloon, seeing nothing, greeting no one. Gunnerson followed with the bottle in the crook of his arm. Even in the shade of the portico the sunlight was blinding as they stepped out of the dark saloon onto the rough board sidewalk. Willy took a moment to get his bearings, then headed south.

Gunnerson grabbed him by the arm. "Hold on. Where're we going?"

Willy seemed to have reached a decision. "I brung the buckboard inta town this mornin' t'pick up some feed for my cows an' chickens. Y'got a horse?"

"Yeah," Gunnerson replied. "Over there. Rented it up at the Benson stable."

"The one right across the street from the depot there?"

"That's the one."

Willy shook his head. "They surely charged y' dearly. I know a place just outta town there where ya could'a *bought* yerself a good mount for the same price those bandits prob'ly charged t'rent you one. Oh well, what's done's done." Willy thought it over. "Y'kin meet me down the road 'bout a mile. There's a big mesquite bosque there."

Gunnerson raised his eyebrows.

"Don't wanna raise no suspicions with the town'folk. After that, y'kin ride with me, if y'want. Tie that expensive horse of yours t'the back o'the wagon."

"How far are we going?"

"'Bout ten miles west a'here. A little less, maybe. I got a small spread down on the San Pedro, north o' Junction City. If y'come up the river, y'prob'ly rode right by it on the way t'Tombstone." He paused. "Which brings up another thing's been a'burrin' me a lot."

"What's bothering you?"

"Well . . . jus' how come you ended up here in Tombstone today anyway?"

The lawyer grinned down at his companion. "I'm surprised a clever fellow like you hasn't figured that out yet."

Willy considered it a bit, then shook his head. "No sir, I ain't. But I got a suspicion."

"Well, your suspicion's probably right, Willy. I was looking for you. And that's the little secret I was celebrating. I found you. That's why I'm here in Tombstone, pardner."

4

On the way to the ranch, with Gunnerson's pinto tied to the back rail, Willy opened up again. "I had nothin' but bad luck since that day I was a'tellin' y'about. Yeah, a long run o' bad luck."

"Tell me about it."

So he told Gunnerson about his little rancho on the river. His daddy had squatted on the land long before the war. And he and his family worked it until one night he failed to come home. Probably killed by scavenging Indians. Probably Chiracahuas. But they never found his body. Or his horse. Willy and his mother and his younger brother managed to scrape by raising and selling a few cattle and farming just enough corn and squash and beans to keep themselves fed. They hired their neighbor Hernando Hernandez to help out with the cattle and chores. He was the oldest son of a Mexican rancher who worked the next spread down the river. They paid him mostly with produce and beef and what little extra cash they might have after a cattle sale. Hernando's children helped out too, more and more as the years wore by. There were seven of them. Three girls and four boys. Good boys and a fine, hard-working crew, they were. After Willy's mother passed and his brother ran off to Texas, Willy managed the ranch by himself, with the help of Hernando and his boys, until Willy got a job driving the mail wagon. It was mostly up and down the San Pedro between Tucson and Tombstone. That provided enough money for Willy to marry a Mexican gal named Maria Cantrell. She and Willy had themselves one son and named him Billy. Actually, it was William José Crandyke, the first name after Willy, and the second after his wife's father still living down in Chihuahua. Those were fine times. Billy was growing into a real joy and a sound ranch hand.

As he talked, Willy opened a wooden box between the seat springs and offered Gunnerson some hard cheese and smoked jerky and cold tortillas.

The lawyer tore off a strip of the jerky and tasted it. "That's different. Kind of musky. And a little on the tough side."

"Yeah. Makes it last on a long haul." Willie laughed. "Until yer jaws give out, that is."

"What kind of meat is it? Venison?"

"No, sir. Javelina. Oh, an' I should warn ya. Bite down real careful like. May be a stray shotgun pellet'r two in there."

They rode in silence for a while until Gunnerson observed, "That doesn't sound like such bad luck to me. Sounds like a very pleasant life."

"An' that it was," Willy mused wistfully. "That it was. The bad luck come later." Gunnerson waited for him to continue. And eventually he did. Reluctantly, it seemed. "That stage coach deal I was a'tellin' y'about. Well, that was the turnin' point for me. That's when m'luck started runnin' bad." He told how Old Harlan had gotten sick and died soon after. Then his boy Billy passed away from a fever. A dark cloud seemed to settle over the ranch. Then his wife decided to visit her family down in Chihuahua and never came back. "There'uz nothing left for her here, I reckon."

Willy stopped talking and they rode in silence.

5

At a wide place in the trail Willy reined the horses to a halt, jumped down, and wrestled open a Texas wire gate. After he drove through, Gunnerson closed the gate behind them. Down the road a short distance stood a sleek thoroughbred mare, saddled and alert, tied to a mesquite branch beside the path. The horses all whinnied back and forth at one another.

"Hernando!" Willy called out. "Somebody I'd like y'ta meet."

A tall, slender Mexican stepped out from the brush. He was dressed in a white cotton shirt and trousers, dirty and stained with sweat. On his feet he wore sandals. His hair was jet black under a broad straw sombrero, but age seemed to tug downward on his brown, wrinkled face.

Willy turned to Gunnerson. "This here's my friend Hernando I was a'tellin' y'bout. Owns the next rancho down the river. Hernan, this here's Mr. Gunnerson. He's a railroad lawyer."

"*Buenos dias, senior. Mucho gusto.*" Hernando doffed his sombrero and bowed.

"Pleased to meet you, Hernando."

"I was a'plannin' t'show Mister Gunnerson here our usual river hospitality, Hernan," Willy grinned. "Say, is everything okay here? Was y'able t'weed out that rough patch a' garden?"

"*Si, senior. He terminado. Ya me voy.*"

"He says he's just leaving," Willy said to Gunnerson. Then to Hernando, "*Adios. Hasta mas tarde.*"

They passed the privy in the dry white dirt and mesquite and greasewood, between a paloverde and a blooming ocotillo. At the end of the road the ranch house rested in the shade of the large cottonwoods which lined the high east bank of the San Pedro. The structure was compact and primitive, built of unpainted boards and battens. In back was a substantial barn, a lean-to shed, and a separate blackened smoke house. Behind that, choked by brush, stood the relic of an old abandoned adobe building, part of its roof missing. A hitching post stood in front of the ranch house. Beside it was a hand pump and a water trough, which the drays found and drank from. A covered porch contained a stack of firewood and a half-dozen cats milling about, tails straight up in the air, waiting to be fed.

"Get out the way," Willy barked at the cats as he led the way inside. The front door opened into a kitchen with a potbelly cooking stove, a table and three chairs, a sideboard with a bucket, a pitcher, and a washtub, and a freestanding larder with open shelves above. An interior door led to a separate bedroom. It was all clean and tidy. "Lemme put a pot a'coffee on and feed these dang cats," he said. "Sit yourself down whilst I put things aright."

Gunnerson eased himself down at the table. "Nice place you've got."

"Uh. It serves." Willy broke some kindling into the stove and lit it, then dumped five big measures of coffee into a pot, tossed in some egg shells, added water with a ladle from the bucket, and set the pot atop the stove. "While she's a'cookin', I reckon I'll offload the hay an' feed an' put the team away." He tipped some warm milk from the pitcher into a saucer and carried it out for the cats.

"I'll give you a hand," Gunnerson said.

Gunnerson untied his horse from the wagon, and while Willy drove back to the barn, he watered the animal at the trough and removed the saddle and draped it over the hitching post. Then Gunnerson led his horse back and helped Willy haul the bales of hay and chicken feed onto a rack inside. They each removed their tack and led their horses by halter into separate empty stalls, lured by flakes of hay and a handful of oats tossed inside. Willy threw out some feed and scratch for the chickens. By the time they got back to the house, the coffee was steaming.

Willy poured two cups. "Sit on down," Willy told his guest. "I'll be back after I use the privy."

Gunnerson blew across the cup and tasted the coffee. It was black and strong.

Willy returned sooner than expected. He was toting a short-barreled, single-shot shotgun in the crook of his right arm. He sidled around Gunnerson as he sat sipping coffee and broke the gun open and checked the load. He spun the cartridge.

"That the same shotgun you were carrying when you were dry-gulched up at Apache Pass?" Gunnerson asked.

"Sure enough is," Will replied. "The very same." He snapped the shotgun shut and raised the barrel and leveled it across the small table at Gunnerson's chest. "Now, suppose you 'splain t'me why I shouldn' jus' kill ya' outright an' forget y'ever came by here."

Gunnerson smiled and shook his head. "Willy, I know you're smarter than that."

"Y'don't look t'be carryin' no weapon. Am I right?"

"That's right."

"Y'got some *secret* weapon, do ya?"

"Nothing secret about it." He held up one finger. "My weapons are my words." He held up a second finger. "And the fact that you are a reasonable man." He held up the third. "And the law is my weapon."

Willy snorted. "Th'ain't no law out here. Not down on this little rancho. Here *I'm* the law." He thought about it. "An' as far as my bein' a *reasonable* man . . . well . . . that just' might be . . . but right this minute my reason's a'tellin' me that the best dang thing I could do t'put all this behind me is t'shoot you dead on the spot an' bury y'down by the river. An' that'll be the end of it." He thought some more. "So I guess that leaves jus' them words o' yours t'deal with. An' I figure y'better start spittin'em out and perty quick."

Gunnerson didn't seem particularly troubled having the scattergun pointed at him. "Willy, there's no reason why you'd want to shoot me."

"Why d'ya say not?"

"For one thing, you'll end up swinging from the end of a rope. Just like Tillman."

Willy shook his head. "They'd never find your body."

"Yes they would. The railroad agents would find it. And they'd find you. Think about it. Everyone at the Crystal Palace saw us together. The link between you and me and Tillman is well known now to a lot of people you don't want to get crossways with. *They* know why I came here. And those railroad agents are pretty tough customers. They would find you out real fast."

Willy thought about it. "I'm still a'listenin'." The shotgun never wavered.

"And besides . . . what would it advantage you to kill me? Just the opposite, I propose. Willy, you *need* me. You need me to decipher the documents in that satchel. I'm the one to do it. Nobody else can. And I can protect you from being prosecuted for taking them in the first place." He paused. "But I already told you that."

"Anythin' else?"

"Yeah, you'd be making a hell of a mess in your kitchen."

"Y'got a point there," Willy nodded. "But I' cleaned up worse.

Butcher my own meat, I do. Is 'at all?"

"No. There's one more thing. I'm betting that you and Old Harlan wanted to strike it rich with that satchel. Well . . . now maybe you can. It's too late for Harlan. And it depends on what I find out when I get a look at those papers. But if they're what I think they are, we may yet turn this into a little bit of a bonanza. For you and me, pardner."

The gun barrel wavered. Then it drooped. "All those years ago . . . I should a' jus' let them robbers have it. It was all for nothin'. I knew Tillman, all right. But I didn't own up t'havin' that satchel. I swore t' him . . . I swore t'him *on my son's life . . . on Billy's life* . . . I swore t'him that I didn't know what he was talkin' about or where that blasted satchel was. An' he believed me. He believed me 'cause I swore on my only son's life." The shotgun slipped from his fingers and thumped on the floor boards against the wall.

Gunnerson said nothing. He made no move.

Willy looked at him with damp eyes. "Y'see, Harlan an' me figured this might be our big chance t'get a foot up. Like you say, maybe t'strike it rich. That satchel must've been worth somethin'. An' we had the robbers and the Injuns and the Mexicans all to blame for havin' took it. The passengers didn't know no different. They was witnesses to it all. An' they backed us up. But when we got back home . . . when we got back home, we was ascared. We couldn't read a word o' that Mexican lingo and had no idea what we had got. And that's when Harlan took sick and died and I was afeared for anybody t'find out what we had done." He swayed a bit. "An' then Billy took the fever an' died too. An' Maria gave me up an' headed back t'Mexico. It all happened so fast. And the whole world changed . . . jus' 'cause Harlan and me did what we did. *I wish t'God we'd a' never a'done it!*"

"Well," Gunnerson said softly, "it's time to turn this thing around for you, don't you think? Time for you to let loose of that wildcat you're been swinging around by the tail all these years. Let's go have a look at those papers and see what we've got." He rose slowly from the table.

Willy didn't move. "You said somethin' about a hun'erd dollars. Jus' t'look at 'em"

Gunnerson smiled. "You're absolutely right. I *did* say that." He reached into his coat pocket and pulled out a roll of ten ten-dollar bills and unfolded them out onto the table. "Earnest money, Willy. That's what we call it. Just to take a look. Yours to keep. And there'll be plenty more if I see what I think I'm going to see."

Willy shook his head slowly. "Seems t'me that *two*-hundred dollars would be a more likeable number for that there up front earnin' money. Before y'get a look at them papers."

"I'm sorry, Willy. And I agree with you. I would be glad to give you another hundred if I had it with me. But I don't. I never ride with that much cash. But here's what I'll do. I will promise you the second hundred, and even put it in writing. I'll give you a note for it. Yours to keep, whatever happens."

Willy's head had not stopped shaking.

"You can't get blood out of a turnip," the lawyer added, raising empty hands. "It's the best offer I can make. Take it or leave it."

Willy stepped over, picked up the bills, and stuck them in his front pocket. "I'll find a pencil an' a piece a'paper. An' let's make it another *two* hun'erd if'n y'gonna do it this away."

6

Willy led him through the brush to the old adobe structure partially concealed by the weeds and greasewood. The path had not been used for a long time. The walls were worn down by weather to expose the pea gravel and rock in the adobe blocks. The main rise of the roof had collapsed long ago. A board and a stack of bricks capped the old adobe chimney. A weathered wooden door hung askew on one good hinge. Willy pushed it open and held it for Gunnerson.

It was dark inside, but Willy knew where he was going. He stepped over to the fireplace and with an "Oomph" dropped to his knees and reached up into the smoke shelf inside. After fiddling for a while, he brought down a small iron-strap strongbox with a splint of wood nailed to the back and left side. In faded letters Gunnerson could just read the words "Wells & Fargo."

"Nice," said the lawyer. "That'll keep the rain off."

"An' the wood rats out. Give me a hand with this, will ya?"

Together they lifted the box and, backing and grunting, Willy led the way out the door. "Seems t'get heavier every damn' year."

"Where'd you get the box?" Gunnerson asked, shouldering his way through.

"Had't a long time. Fell off'n a stage up in Tombstone an' broke, an' they didn't want it no more. So I says, 'I'll take it,' and they guv it t'me. I patched her up."

Outside, clear of the brush, they plopped the box into the dirt and Willy swung it open. He drew out an oilskin cloth and carefully unwrapped it. "This wha'cha a'lookin' for?" He held out the polished leather of the finely scrolled Mexican satchel.

Gunnerson took it gingerly and admired the tool work. "Let's take it inside, Willy, and see what we've got here."

Willy watched from across the room as Gunnerson slowly turned the pages from an unread pile to a read one. He didn't say much as he read. Outside the low sun flickered and flashed through the cottonwood leaves and branches as it settled toward the mountains.

"Well?" Willy would ask.

But the lawyer would only hold up his hand and mutter, "Just a minute."

When Gunnerson had turned the final page, he looked up and smiled. "This is the real thing, Willy. These are the original Mexican land grant deeds. This is what the railroad has been looking for."

Willy moved to the edge of the table. "But I got a question for ya. These here deeds, or whatever they are, well, they could affect the title t'*my* land, couldn't they?"

"You're a homesteader? You've got title issued under the Homestead Act?"

"Yes, I do. And so does Hernando down river."

"Is Hernando an American citizen?"

"Yes sir, he's a citizen. Natural-born in the New Mexico Territory. Now, what I'm askin' is, could these here sheets a'paper take our land away from us?"

"Well . . . only if they happen to cover the same ground. The same piece of land. I can't determine that right now. We would need to hire a surveyor for that. But it's not very likely. The chances are small."

"But the Mexican grants got priority?"

"*Priority?* Where'd you pick up a fancy word like that, Willy?"

"Well . . . matter a'fact . . . I had'em looked at once before. This fella happened t'come by an' *he* seemed t'think these here deeds would take our land away from us. Me an' Hernando, too. Is'at true?"

Gunnerson squinted at the cowboy with a new appreciation. And concern. "We don't know that, Willy."

"But it could all be took away."

"Well . . . I don't think that's very likely."

"But it *could be*?"

"No . . . no, that's not really possible. These all apply to land lying elsewhere."

"Where?"

"Over near Patagonia, for one. See here . . ." Gunnerson shuffled for a particular deed. "See here? This land lies southwest of Patagonia." He picked up another one. "And this one is down by Babocomari . . . and this one is over by Fort Huachuca . . ."

"That ain't very far away."

"No . . . no, but–"

"So you're a'tellin' me that this other fellow was a'lyin' t'me?"

Gunnerson stopped talking and considered for a moment. "No, Willy, I'm not saying that. We just need more information before we can reach any sort of conclusion." He stood. Arched his back. "All this excitement has got my bowels stirred up. Where's that privy of yours."

Gunnerson was only gone long enough to take something out of his saddlebag hanging over the rail outside. He slowly pushed the door open a crack. Willy was sitting at the table trying to understand the deeds spread out there. The shotgun still lay on the other side of the room where it had fallen. Gunnerson pushed the door open all the way with his left hand. In his right was a Colt .45 revolver pointed at the cowboy.

Willy looked up and smiled. "I thought so," he said. "*Dang!* Looks like you was a'plannin' t'take these papers with ya all along."

"That's right. Put them all back into the satchel. Slowly." He stepped around Willy, picked up the shotgun, broke it open, dumped out the shell, came back and tossed it out the door. "Just in case you get any crazy ideas."

"I thought you said we was gonna be pardners," Willy said as he shuffled the documents carefully back into the satchel. "When d'y'plan on payin' me my share?"

"Your share," Gunnerson laughed. "Those deeds don't belong to you. Never did. Why should I pay you anything?"

"This ain't right."

"What are you gonna do, sue me?" he laughed again. "And while I'm thinking about it, you better give me back that hundred dollars I laid out as earnest money."

Willy shook his head. "Ain't got it."

"Stand up. Turn out you pockets."

Willy did so. They were empty.

"I'll shoot you."

"No, y'won't. Hernando saw you. Heard me say your name. Killin' me would be a whole lot mor'n a hun'erd dollars worth a'trouble t'ya." Willy didn't blink.

"Just give me the damned satchel then."

Willy handed it to him.

"Now, saddle up my horse while I keep an eye on you."

7

Willy watched him ride off. The sun had dropped below the Huachuca peaks in the west, but an almost-full moon had already risen over the Tombstone Hills. He entered the ranch house and took off his big hat, brushing the thin whisps of graying hair back over his ears. He lit a kerosene lamp and poured himself another cup of lukewarm coffee, then sat down at the table where Gunnerson had spread out the documents. Willy was smiling.

He didn't have to wait long before the sharp crack of a Winchester rifle echoed through the cottonwoods along the San Pedro. It was followed quickly by another. Willy sipped his coffee and continued his vigil. Then came the final rifle crack, the coup de grace, and it was finished. Willy drew in a deep breath and let it out slowly, satisfied.

He waited for over an hour. But Willy was not impatient. Hernando had a lot of work to do. Finally he heard hoofbeats and carried the lantern out onto the porch. The moon was well up, and in the bright moonlight Hernando led Gunnerson's riderless pinto down the long driveway. When they got closer, he could see the Mexican satchel swinging from the pommel of Hernando's horse. "How'd it go, Hernan?" Willy asked, raising the lantern.

"Not too bad," Hernando responded. "Jus' like before."

Willy nodded. "How many is that now? Five?"

"No. *Yo creo que* six."

"That many."

"*Si*. Countin' the Butterfield agent."

"Oh, yeah, plum' forgot 'bout him. The very first one. Didn't make any profit on that one." Willy grinned. "We couldda started our own grave yard business, Hernan. Whadda y'think about that?"

"*Ejoles!* You need somebody else do the digging."

Willy laughed. "Did Gunnerson have any more cash in those saddlebags a'his?"

"*Si*. I count out more than eight-hundred dollars. But it was dark. Might be more."

"Why that cheapskate dirty lyin' son-of-a-gun thief! He tol' me a hun'erd was all he had with 'im." Willy laughed again. "Guess he thought he didn't need t'show the rest a'that bankroll t'take advantage of this poor ol' broke-down stage driver."

Hernando laughed with him. "We do pretty good."

"Yeah we did. Marshall 'll want his cut, a'course. Always does."

"*Por supuesto*. But we no need tell him how much we got. Or about the horse."

Willy thought it over. "Sell the horse to the Apaches?"

"I can do that, *senior*." Hernando handed down the satchel and dismounted.

"Well . . . come on inside. I'll cook us up another pot a'coffee."

Hernando smiled. "*Si, gracias, compañero*."

Willy slapped him on the back. "Y'got that right, Hernan. Pardners."

The People's Will

In the Spring of 1969 I was renting the lower flat in an old house on College Avenue in Berkeley. I had finished law school and was preparing to take the bar exam across the bay in San Francisco. The apartment was just two blocks away from what was to become the Peoples Park fiasco. So when I needed a study break, I would naturally mosey on over to see what the hell was going on.

Frankly, I was more of an observer than a participant. I couldn't have cared less about the power of the people to commandeer unused land owned by the mighty University of California for a public garden and park. It all seemed a bit overblown. And at the rallies on the steps of Sproul Plaza, those who spoke so vehemently on behalf of "the People" seemed to me more enamored with their own oratory than with the advancement of civilization or social justice.

The huge vacant field itself was unremarkable. The April sunshine had dried the mud and the ruts. A few rusty relics of abandoned autos were strewn randomly on the dusty tract. In the clouds of sepia-toned dust toiled an army of peasant workers, looking like specters from an old communist propaganda newsreel. No law enforcement was in evidence. (In the beginning, before it turned ugly, the city fathers and the university had adopted a hands-off policy, while they wrestled with the improbable task of charting a safe passage between the whirlpool of anarchy and the unyielding shoal of the new governor in Sacramento.)

The workers were building a community vegetable garden. A big one. A leaderless army of peasants was digging with shovels and rakes and hoes and buckets, heaping the soil into long rows of mounds. The raised beds were for tilling and planting. The furrows in between would provide irrigation. The peoples's army seemed to act as one body, with one unspoken voice, one movement, one revolution, devoid of generals or captains or even squad leaders to taint the purity of the people's will.

But then, through the dust, came the one figure I remember. The one figure I can't seem to forget. He was a skinny black guy whose name I never knew. I think of him as "Leroy." Leroy shuffled toward me down one of the new rows, shoveling dirt from the new-built mounds back into the flood trench. Slowly he advanced. Patiently. Laboriously. The crunch of his shovel in the loose mound and the plop of the soil splaying back into the swale accompany his frail figure in my memory. His face was gaunt and his figure slight. He appeared younger than the others, the college students. Perhaps he was still in high school. I cannot remember what he wore, only that it was coated with the pale dust that filled the air. Shovelful after shovelful, Leroy was fulfilling his own vision of what needed to be done.

Fascinated, I watched to see what would be done about Leroy. Who would take action? And by what authority? *Ca-chunk . . . ca-chunk*, shovel by shovel, Leroy proceeded toward me, turned, and started back on the next row. People frowned. They clustered together and shook their heads. Finally a young man with his own shovel fell in behind Leroy to scoop up the soil Leroy had thrown down and return it to the planting mound. As far as I saw, no one spoke to Leroy. No one attempted to *correct* him. In the seeds of such a correction, I began to see, would be the unraveling of the entire collective will. The People's Will. So, to the collective eye, Leroy had to remain invisible.

A few days later Governor Reagan, acting out his own political fantasy, sent in the highway patrol and local police and sheriffs' deputies to put down the insurrection, and when they were unable to manage, he called down the hordes of National Guard troops in full battle gear like locusts. The whole debacle was interesting, even captivating at times, but it flared and faded for me as another empty pyrotechnic flash in the crazily unfolding universe. I do not recall the names of the young men killed and blinded by buckshot from police shotguns. Nor do I recall the smell of tear gas. Nor the mass arrests. Nor the color of the sprigs of flowers that smiling young girls stuck into the barrels of bayoneted rifles. None of it provoked me enough to nag at the strings of my memory almost half a century later. Except for Leroy. It is Leroy alone who has ridden down these many years with me.

I have since encountered the "will of the people" on a wearisome number of occasions. As the years wore by, I assumed the duties of city attorney in a small town in northern California. There, trapped like a rat at city council meetings, I would endure some bombastic bore from the audience demanding that all dogs be on leash. Or that the leash law be revoked and animals allowed to run free. Someone else wanted to see more police on the streets. Yet another decried the excessive number of police officers in town. Or that the parks and recreation budget needed to be increased. Or decreased. But always, *always*, it was on behalf of "the people" that they advocated.

And I would draw a breath, and settle back in my chair, and close my eyes. Leroy would be there, approaching through the dust, *ca-chunk* . . . *ca-chunk*, shovelful after shovelful, declaring by his contrariety that he too was of the people, and that he had a vision of his own.

The Woodsman

1

Bilford's cough broke the rhythm of the night. Frogs fell silent. He bent forward and felt for the poker stick beneath his log, found it, and jabbed at the campfire, sending a cloud of sparks billowing into the heavens. The fire crackled. Branches overhead flickered like the holy arches of a cathedral. He cleared his throat and spat into the flames. "Anybody got the time?"

The question roused Anders to take another mouthful of Yukon Jack from the fifth he cradled in his arms. "The fuck difference does it make?" Nolan Anders was slender and pale. His short blond hair and prematurely balding pate gave him the look of a mendicant friar. He was obviously drunk as a skunk. As were they all. "Za' matter a' fac', I got all the time in the world." He chuckled. "Time's 'bout *all* I got."

Bilford chewed on that for a bit. He was a burly beast of a man. Curly black hair grew from his head and face and arms and legs like an old circus bear. "You *got* time, huh? Whazzat s'posed t'mean? Y'*got* time?"

"I got plen'y a' time. Here, take this fuckin' thing, will ya?" Anders held out the bottle.

Bilford took it and downed a burning slug. "Yeah," he croaked. "But . . . what *is* it ya *got*?"

"Time."

"The hell *is* time, anyhow?"

Anders tried to recollect something clever he'd once read. "Time . . . wait . . . time's what . . . time's what keeps everything from happenin' all at once."

Bilford spat into the fire again. "How the fuck could ever'thing happen all at once?" he snorted. "S'too simple. Time's a process. Time is . . . a process. Can't have a fuckin' process without time."

Anders nodded in agreement. "It'd be chaos."

"Can't even have no chaos. Chaos takes time. Time t' happen."

Anders sighed. After a while he gave it another try. "Time's jus' the shit we slog through ever' fuckin' day. S'the swamp we live in."

"Uh," Bilford grunted without commitment.

"Right, Rucker?" Anders called. "Yer the fuckin' philosophizer. Rucker?"

They peered into the unlit void behind the big fir where a yellow strand of poly rope was tied. An invisible hammock creaked, and Rutlan Rucker's knees and hands and face materialized into the flickering light as he planted both feet in the duff. His hair was wild and yellower than the firelight. His ruddy face was stubbled with whiskers. "Gentlemen," he said, "I hate t'piss on your parade, but you are both wrong." He tried to stand up, but a button halfway up his sleeve caught in the cords and yanked him back into the hammock. Tumbling and laughing, he managed to right himself again. "And if one of you gentlemen . . . would be kind enough to walk that bottle of whiskey over here . . . where this cunning hammock is holding me prisoner . . . I will explain to you the error of your ways."

Bilford grunted to his feet, stubbing his toe on the end of a fire log, which spit tracers of glowing embers between his feet. He tap danced away, caught and steadied himself against the tree trunk, then lurched around it with the almost empty bottle. "This better be fucking good," he grumbled.

Rucker accepted the offering and downed its sacrament in one long gulp. The empty bottle slipped from his fingers and clanked onto the rocks. He cleared his throat. "Now, listen up, gentlemen. What you call 'time' . . . is but a tool by which consciousness organizes the world."

Tottering, Bilford waited for more. But that seemed to be it. "The fuck zat s'posed t'mean?"

"Yeah," demanded Anders with a derisive belch, "whadda you know about it, mister smarty-ass professor?"

"S'a simple matter of fact," rejoined Rucker loudly. "Any dolt can see it plain as the balls on a billy goat. Before the human brain . . . well, shit . . . before *any* nervous system developed . . . there was no time."

They pondered the implications mournfully as the empty bottle sparkled in the firelight.

"Time," Rucker continued, when he thought they were ready, "s'a trick. A tool. Na'llusion. Nothin' more'n a cerebral process by which consciousness optimizes its own benefit." He paused for his words to sink in.

After a while Bilford muttered, "That's pure bullshit, Rucker."

"Yeah, this is stupid," Anders added, easing himself down onto the ground against a granite boulder. "S'makin' me dizzy. Bring on the dancin' girls. Before I pass out."

"Aw, who wants t'talk this fucking philosophy shit, anyhow?" Bilford groused, stumping back to his log seat. "Hurts my head." He thumped down a little too fast and nearly pitched over backward.

"But . . ." Rucker continued, ignoring their jibes and raising an imperious finger, ". . . we have gone *way* too far with it. With all our clocks an' calendars and beeps an' boops an' integrated circuits an' . . . whatever . . . we have *objectified* time. Now it's a fuckin' god. An' we serve it like slaves. An' it's not even fuckin' *real*."

"Go back to sleep, Rucker. Me 'n Anders gotta figure out where we gonna catch us some fish tomorrow."

"See," persisted Rucker. "There y'go . . . *planning*. Just proves my point."

"Ain't none is this lake."

"Planning and remembering," Rucker went on, "are the birth of time. Now, can you tell me just how is it that you are able to *plan* at all?"

"Sos we can catch us some fuckin' *fish*, that's why."

"Not *why*," Rucker countered. "*How?*"

"*Jesus!* How the fuck do I know? Ask Anders. He's a city planner. That's what he fuckin' *does* for a livin'. Planning. Tell him, Anders."

Anders's sleepy voice floated like an echo from the granite slab against which he was slumped. "Tell 'im whut?"

"How you *plan*. Haven't you been listenin'?"

"Yeah . . . uh, no . . . maybe I . . . uh . . . mighta dozed off there for jus' a second."

"Tell Rucker how ya plan things."

"How I *plan* things?" He struggled unsuccessfully to straighten his spine against the striated rock.

"Yeah. Rucker wants to know how ya *plan*."

"Well . . . geez . . . I dunno . . . never thought 'bout it. Jus' comes natural. Habit."

"Whaddaya do as a city planner?" asked Rucker.

"*Deputy* city planner . . . *chief* deputy planner . . . what? . . . well . . . guess I research . . . an' manipulate things . . . ideas . . . n'order t'chief . . . t'chief . . . whazza wurt?"

"Achieve," Rucker prompted.

"Yeah, 'at's'it . . . 'chieve . . . a desirable . . . future."

"There y'go, Rucker," Bilford crowed. "Z'at what y'were lookin' for?"

"It'll do jus' fine. See? That's time in action. The origin of the future."

"Bullshit."

"No more'n anything else. 'S'all cerebral."

They sat in silence for a while before Anders announced, "I'm cold."

"Why'n't ya just crawl inta yer sleepin' bag?" Bilford suggested. "Get on in the tent."

"'Cause . . . I think I might be sick . . . things spinning 'round . . . when I close my eyes."

"Jesus! Don't puke in the tent. Go on over there inta the bushes. Jus' stick yer finger down yer throat. Y'ull feel a lot better. Here, me an' yer friend Rucker'll give ya a hand. Rucker! Help me out here, will ya?"

"Coming," Rucker said. "If this fuckin' hammock'll let go a'me."

Switching on their headlamps, Rucker and Bilford each took an arm and half supported and half dragged Anders across the rocky clearing to an overgrowth of azaleas beside the lake. They looked like miners hauling out a sack of coal. Anders gagged along the way and vomited as soon as they put him down.

"Thass good," Bilford encouraged him. "Get it all out."

On his hands and knees Anders coughed and choked and gasped as his stomach clenched with the dry heaves. When the spasms passed, he hung his head, shivering.

Bilford pulled off his hoodie and draped it over Anders' shoulders.

"Now don' get any puke on my sweatshirt or I'll kill ya."

Anders waved them away with a wobbly arm.

"Think he wants a little privacy," Rucker said.

They took a few steps and turned off their headlamps. The bright web of the Milky Way stretched from horizon to horizon across the black dome of moonless sky and stole their thoughts.

After a while Rucker called, "You okay, Andy?"

"Go 'way," Anders muttered from the darkness.

"Alright," Bilford said. "We'll be back in a while t' see how yer doin'."

"Need anything?" Rucker asked.

"Water." Anders spat.

"Where's your canteen?"

No reply

"We'll find it."

They turned and crunched back toward the campfire by the light of Rucker's headlamp. "S'funny," Bilford said, "but I don't feel particularly drunk any more."

"S'a hell of a thing," Rucker agreed. "So, how do you know Andy?"

"AA."

"Alcoholics Anonymous?"

"Yup. Long time ago. He was my sponsor. Still is."

"But . . . ." Rucker slackened his stride.

"Yeah, yeah, I know. Sounds weird. But we tie one on together once a year. S'hard t'explain. Climbin' inta the mouth of the beast. Celebratin' our imperfection. Kind of a Zen thing."

Rucker thought about it. "Y'still go to meetings?"

"Most weeks." He grinned. "Missin' one tonight, though."

"I'll bet. Do the others know?"

"I got no secrets. From them'r anybody else."

"Whadda they think about your . . . unorthodox approach?"

Bilford laughed. "Whaddaya think?"

They arrived at camp and Bilford criss-crossed a couple of sticks and a small log on top of the glowing embers. Then he bent down onto one knee and blew it to life.

Rucker settled onto the log where Anders had been sitting. "Y'want the hammock?"

"Hell no," Bilford groaned, settling onto his own log. "I saw what the fucker did to you. Jus' like a pitcher plant an' a fly. Anyhow, I could warm these bones a little while we wait."

"Gettin' cold," Rucker agreed and leaned in toward the fire.

After a while Bilford said, "Y'know, what you were sayin' earlier, 'bout cerebral time an' plannin'? Got me t'thinkin' 'bout something."

After a silence, Rucker prompted, "What's that?"

"Oh . . . jus' . . . when I started out practicin' law, way back when—"

"You're a lawyer?"

"Yeah. Was anyway. Night school. Before they disbarred me. Anyway, I did a lotta criminal defense work. Way back when. Small stuff. Misdemeanors. Traffic shit. Wobbler felonies I'd bargain down t' misdemeanors."

"Can't picture you in front of a jury," Rucker interjected.

"No. You got that right. Jury'd likely toss *me* in jail. Mostly I'd plead 'em out, one way or another. Jury work was jus' too crazy. Didn't pay. Never knew what might happen. An' it took too long. Made my money turning 'em over fast as I could. A couple hundred bucks a pop." They sat in silence for a while before Bilford continued, "Anyway, that talk about plannin' got me t' thinkin'. Mosta my clients jus' wanted me t' put their case over another month. Get a continuance. Even a coupla weeks would do. Anything. Worry 'bout it later."

"Procrastination."

"Yup. They jus' didn't wanna fuckin' *deal* with it now. A couple more weeks on the street was all they could see as a goal in life."

"Even the innocent?"

Bilford barked out a laugh. "Innocent? None of 'em was ever innocent. I'm not sayin' they were *bad*. No. They were mostly sad sacks who jus' couldn't figure out how t' live in society. Made stupid choices, not understandin' the consequences. An' the system didn't have room for 'em. The DA didn't have time t' bother with 'em. My job was t'get the best deal I could work out for 'em and move on."

"Any women?"

"Oh yeah, there were some. Pretty down and out. Mostly prostitutes. Drunk drivers. Suspended licenses. Weed was big back then. Not like the meth today. Evil stuff."

The conversation faltered.

"Procrastination," Rucker muttered, mostly to himself.

"Yup."

They fell silent.

"You say this was before you were disbarred?"

"Course it was."

"What was that about? If you don't mind my asking."

"Nah. That came a few years later. After I'd moved up t' trusts an' estates. I had a nasty cocaine habit then. Borrowed some money from a client's trust account. Went straight up my nose. Didn't think the old biddy would miss it. But her accountant did."

Rucker waited for more. "Did you do any jail time?"

"No. They dropped charges when I paid the money back. I spent a coupla days in county jail is all. Then the state bar court offered me my license back if I'd jump through their hoops. But I was tired of it all by then. That whole life. Jus' let 'em take it."

2

A mosquito whined in his ear and he slapped himself awake. Anders was cold. Rocks dug painfully into his arm and hip. He was lying on his side. He struggled back onto his hands and knees. The movement spun his head. He wretched and coughed, but nothing more came up.

Where the hell are they with my water bottle?

He was thirsty. More than thirsty. He ached to wash the putrid bile out of his mouth. From deep in his throat. It was gagging him. Defiling him. He longed for purification.

But he had to stop dozing like this. Had to help himself out. He pulled on Bilford's sweatshirt and zipped it up.

He could smell water. Could hear it trickling. Close by. They had dumped him on the shore. Oh, he couldn't *drink* lake water. Not with giardia. But he could rinse out his mouth. His throat. Had to do that. Couldn't wait any longer.

So Anders crawled forward into the thicket. Pushing along an animal trail he could not see. But he could feel it. A rabbit trail. Toward the water he heard tinkling. Smelled the damp soil. It couldn't be far. He punched through scraping, clasping brush. Sharp rocks pricked his palms and knees. Stiff branches tore back his hood. Bushes scraped his shoulders. Scratched his neck. His wrists. He felt insects crawling in his hair. Down his neck. Spiders, he thought. Ticks. But he had to reach water. Head down, he ploughed onward. And onward. Finding water was everything.

He broke through into a dim opening. He could make out the pale splashes of granite rocks. The dark silhouettes of trees. A star-bright sky. Unfolding himself from his low cringe, Anders rose unsteadily to his feet, brushing the bugs out of his hair with his hands. He shook out the sweatshirt, then tugging it back on and zipped it tight around his neck. *If I puke on it, Bilford will kill me.*

When the lightheadedness lifted, he raised his eyes to the starlit landscape. He saw no lake. No shoreline. No lapping waves. Nothing to slake his thirst. *Shit!* He had not studied the map. That he had left for Bilford. And Rucker. They loved maps. That was their thing. He hadn't bothered to orient himself. Now he had gotten himself turned around. With no sense of direction back to camp.

But he *could* hear water. Above him. Tinkling. Gurgling. A stream. Inlet or outlet? It made no difference. In a protective crouch, he started climbing a rocky, brushy slope toward the sound. Low scrub slashed at his bare shins. Pebbles caught painfully in his sandals. But at least the uphill scramble brought warmth. *Time is distance*, he thought as he climbed. *Each step is a moment. The moments add up to the distance to water. Distance and motion. Time.*

He was panting and sweating by the time he crested a berm with a small ravine beyond. Mosquitoes whined about his head. The ground dropped steeply through cobble-sized rocks. He stumbled down to the bottom, where his feet splashed into a narrow stream. He fell on his knees and sucked up a mouthful of water. It was cold and delicious. He washed his throat and spit it out. Gargling felt like a long overdue laugh. He swished out his mouth. And then, almost involuntarily, he drank deeply. Like a horse. On all fours. He couldn't help himself. The water churned in his stomach, considered coming back up, then decided to settle there. After a few moments he felt better than he had in a long while.

Anders stood in the cold water and gazed about. A series of short waterfalls fed the stream with a musical cadence. Far up the slope, at the top of a star-defined ridge, his eye caught the orange glow of a campfire in the branches. It seemed the wrong direction, but tonight he was no navigator. He sloshed out and started up toward the camp. They would be surprised to see him strutting in. Probably didn't even know he had gotten himself lost. No need to tell them. Everything would be fine now.

The climb was long and slow and Anders was spent when he reached the ridge crest. But there was no campfire. The orange-yellow glow that had drawn him was from a gibbous moon just rising on the far horizon ahead. He sighed and hung his head. At least he now knew which way was east.

Mosquitoes were still circling his head, drawn by his exhalations and sweat. A cold breeze cut him from behind. From the west. He was sick and exhausted and lost. All he wanted now was to make it through the night. His best chance was to find shelter, hunker down, and make his way back to camp first thing in the morning. A small pocket meadow in the warm moonlight below looked inviting. It would be out of the wind. He could make out a faint path down to it. Maybe even a trail. And the slope looked gentler than the one he had just climbed. Like a golf course fairway. It would be easy to circle back to camp in the morning.

3

Bilford stood and stretched his back. "Been sittin' too damn long. I'm ready t'turn in. Where the hell's Anders?"

Rucker yawned. "We left him down by the water, remember?"

"Course I remember. But where the hell *is* he?"

Rucker shrugged. "Guess he's still down there. Want me to go fetch him?"

"Jesus. He prob'ly fell asleep. Hope the weasels didn't get'im."

"I can go." Rucker rose and switched on his headlight. "Which one of these water bottles is his?"

Bilford looked around and pointed. "That one."

"Told him I'd bring it to him. Kinda slipped my mind."

"Uh. Shit happens. Guess I'll tag along. What time d'ya think it is?"

"No idea." Rucker grinned. "Andy's the one who's got all the time."

Bilford snickered. "All the time in the world."

They emerged from their secluded grove. The Milky Way was washed out by a yellow glow in the eastern sky. The moon had risen beyond the ridge. Would be rising there soon. They shuffled stiffly across the clearing to the shrubs beside the lake where they had left Anders.

He wasn't there.

"Shit!" spat Bilford. "What the hell? This's where we left'im, i'n't it?"

Rucker swept the ground with his light. "Yeah. That's his puke. And look. See those drag marks. They're fresh. Looks like he dragged himself off that way, into the bushes."

"What the fuck for? *Jesus!* I hope he didn't fall in the lake an' get drownd."

"I'll check the lake," Rucker responded, backtracking to a short brush-choked path to the shore. The ground was muddy with no sign of Anders. "No sign of him over here."

"Nothin' floatin'?"

Rucker swept the water with his light. "No. He's not here."

"Unless he fuckin' sank already."

Rucker broke back into the clearing. "No. No sign of footprints or drag marks that I could see. And look at this. Looks like he was crawling into the brush *away* from the water."

"Ya think, Tonto?"

"Yeah. Looks like it."

"Shit. Why would he do that?"

"*Andy?*" Rucker called tentatively.

No response.

"*Anders!*" Bilford bellowed.

The call echoed off the cliff above the lake. No response.

"*Anders, you motherfucker! Where the fuck are you? This is not funny!*"

"*—not funny,*" came the echo. No response.

Bilford turned to Rucker. "Whadda we gonna do now?"

The brush was too thick to see through. They split up and wandered around calling Anders' name, receiving back nothing but echoes.

When they met again at the clearing, Rucker was worried. "What if he's hurt?"

"More likely he's fuckin' with us." Bilford spat. "Sitting out there somewhere laughin' his ass off."

Rucker shook his head. "Doesn't sound like Andy t'me."

"Or jus' wandered off and got hisself lost. Now *that* sounds more like'im."

"Then why can't he hear us calling? I think he's hurt."

They pondered in silence until Bilford said, "Either way, not much we can do tonight. S'too dark."

"Yeah. Okay. I say we go back to camp and build up the fire. Maybe he'll see it and find his way back on his own. If not, we can get up with first light and do a proper search."

"We'll find'im in the mornin'. Couldn't't've got far."

4

The meadow was not the smooth green golf course that his mind had imagined from above. Deceptive moonlight helped him see some of the pale rocks, but not all of them. And the dark low shrubs were often indistinguishable from their shadows. His ankles wobbled on the rocks and the brush caught his sandals and scarred his legs. The path turned out not to be a path at all, but a narrow, rocky, drought-dry creek bed meandering down the center of the long valley swale. Still woozy and weak, with stubby saddler oak and manzanita trying to trip him, Anders descended blindly down the unsteady rocks. When they shifted beneath his tread, he had to sit down roughly to keep from pitching forward head-over-heels down the slope. He took to counting his steps and his breaths to clock the time and endure the jagged descent.

At last the dry creek bed arrived at an impenetrable thicket of willows, where seeps and springs resurfaced as a sluggish stream. On the marge in the moonlight he found a patch of sword ferns growing from soft black mud. He ripped up an armful and carried them up to a narrow bench between two tall pines. There, in the needles and duff, Anders built himself a nest, spreading out half the ferns for bedding and drawing the rest over his bare legs. He tugged up the hood of the sweatshirt and zipped it tight about his neck. Sick and exhausted, he settled in for the night. The stream tinkled through the willows and soon frogs resumed their croaking.

But sleep eluded him. As soon as he started to doze, a mosquito would whine in his ear. Unseen things crawled on his bare flesh beneath the blanket of ferns. A cold draft wafted down from the ridge far above. All he wanted to do was make it through the night. But time seemed to stand still. *Time*, he mused, trying to recall the conversation at camp. It seemed so long ago. He tried to remember if he had ever spent a more miserable evening, but could think of nothing even close.

He dozed. And he dreamt. His father was angry with him. Looming sternly, he lectured, "You can't do something just because all the *other* kids are doing it. You're not one of *them*. You're an *Anders*. You're *better* than the rest. And you've got to *show* them that." He jerked awake and slapped at a mosquito, boxing his ear. It rang from the slap.

Again he dozed. Bilford was there this time, menacing him. But no. It was not Bilford. It was a beast with wiry black fur and horns sprouting from his head, rising onto its hind legs, displaying an ugly white belly and a writhing grub of pudendum. It was the goat god. The devil. Anders jumped and scratched at something crawling up his leg. He sat up to clear his head. The moon had not moved in the sky.

And he dozed again and awoke brushing crawling things from his hair. Shame engulfed him. Shame that he was lost. Shame that everyone was going to know. He was supposed to be better than this. Better than all the others. But he had gotten himself stupidly lost. Bilford would mock him mercilessly. Rucker might just smile and move on, but he would never be able to face Bilford again.

Anders grew angry. Wrath swelled in his belly with the unclean water. Suddenly he despised Bilford and everything Bilford stood for. Bilford's idea to get roaring drunk tonight. Hair of the dog that bit you. Homeopathic cure. Anders had known better. He liked the wagon, actually. But Bilford had twisted his will, taunting him, as he did year after year.

Anders despised himself most of all. For kowtowing for Bilford's favor all these years. Anders regretted it all. His own frailty. His own drinking. Bilford. Resolutely he sat up. "It stops here and now," he vowed. "All of it."

But the night was long and miserable and episodic. And as Rucker might have told him, the mind which creates time, also erases it. So when the glow of morning finally rousted him from his bed of torment, Anders had mostly forgotten his dreams. And his resolutions.

5

Bilford unzipped the tent fly and squinted a bloodshot eye into the dew-bright dawn. He spotted Rucker blowing into a smoky fire beneath the coffee pot. "The fuck is he?"

Rucker shrugged his shoulders, drew another breath, and blew the fire to life.

"Ya didn't see nothin' down there?"

Favoring the morning quiet, Rucker had taken a solitary walk at first light, making his way down to where they had dumped Anders. For nearly an hour he had tromped through tangled brakes beside the lake, calling out his name. No response. No sign. Nothing at all. "Nope."

"This is unbe*liev*able!" Bilford rocked unsteadily first on one foot and then on the other as he tugged on his trousers. "That inconsiderate son of a whore-bitch! Never came back, did he? Now what the hell'er we s'posed t'do?"

Rucker peeled a strip of bacon into the skillet. "We'll find him."

"Fuck!"

6

Anders awoke cold and sick and woozy, and he didn't know where the hell he was. The light of dawn confused him. Everything looked different. The rocks were all rough and reddish and black. Other than a few tall pines, the trees grew sparse and stunted. Like another world. Where was all the creamy granite? The pale cliff faces and rounded, speckled boulders? He couldn't even spot the ridge he had crested before dropping down into this valley swale. He recognized nothing.

Unsteadily he stood, his left foot throbbing painfully. Far up to his right was a ridge crest. Granite. Not the way he had come, he was pretty sure, but maybe a way to get back. He would have to climb steeply and angle over to that ridge. Maybe he could circle back to camp that way. But the climb would be grueling, especially the way he felt, and the headwall up there looked like it might be impassable.

"*Bilford!*" he yelled at the top of his lungs.

No reply. Not even an echo.

"*Rucker?*"

Nothing.

"*Where the hell are you?*"

The breeze soughed in the pines. The creek tinkled. In the distance a nuthatch beeped and a woodpecker hammered. Otherwise, all was silence.

Fear began to worm its way into his belly. It riled up his bowels. Anders eased himself down on a flat, sharp-edged black slab. His legs were scratched and scabbed. The big toe of his left foot was red and swollen where a thorn had stabbed and broken off beneath the nail. There were welts on the top of his bald head and his skin itched all over. His toe throbbed with his heartbeat. And he was cold. And tired. And thirsty. And still a little queasy in his stomach.

He held his head in his hands, breathed deeply, and tried to collect his thoughts. He could find his own way out of this mess. All by himself. He could do it. It would be crazy to try to find his way back to camp and maybe get lost even worse than he was already. So it didn't really feel like a decision. Or at least one *he* made. It was simply the way things had to be. He would find his own way down to the river. There would be a trail. There was always a trail along a river. And then he would follow the trail downstream to the trailhead. And civilization. He could do that. He was an *Anders*. He'd be out of there by nightfall.

Anders felt bad for Rucker. Rucker would be worried about him. He and Bilford would have to pack out all his stuff as well as their own. Six miles to the trailhead. But, hell, Bilford had carried most of it in to begin with. He was the mountain man. Bilford loved this shit. Roughing it in the wilderness. The more remote the better. And this was all his fault anyway. But he felt bad about Rucker.

7

"Well . . . I'm headin' out," announced Bilford, his thick, curly hair and beard and hirsute arms and legs poking solidly from his T-shirt and walking shorts. He looked like a cartoon Sasquatch paratrooper, with his own pack bulging on his back and Anders' strapped in front and fishing rods and coils of rope and stuff sacks and bottles sprouting in between. He planned to hike down to the car and drive to the nearest town for help. In the meantime Rucker would continue to search around camp. And be there if Anders should find his way back. "Now don't you get yourself lost too."

"Well," Rucker grinned, "with two of us lost, you'd double the chances of finding one of us." His face grew somber. "No, I've got to keep looking. I still think he's lying out there somewhere. Hurt. It's the only way any of this makes sense."

"I still think he might jus' be fuckin' with us." Bilford shifted his eighty-pound burden as lightly as if it weighed half as much.

"You don't really believe that, do you?"

For the first time Rucker saw concern in his companion's eyes. Bilford looked away. "No. Nolan's a city boy. Doesn't have a clue about what t'do out here. In the wilderness. He ain't no woodsman. Doesn't know the first thing about survivin'." He shook his head. "I should never've brought 'im along."

"Don't fret about it. We'll find him. And don't forget to pick me up at the trailhead come nightfall. If I'm not there, it means I've found Anders. Send somebody in to help me with him."

"Aye aye, cap'n." Bilford snapped a mock salute. Then he wheeled and lumbered down the trail, strangely light-footed for his gorilla size.

8

Anders found a narrow, overgrown opening in the willow thicket and pushed his way through, the branches slapping his face and the sedge cutting his shins. In the midst, where the stream crossed, were three round stepping stones. Anders stared at the stones. Someone had placed them there. He was on a *path*. Tears welling in his eyes, he pushed on through and emerged in a darlingtonia fen above a wide wet meadow on the other side. He recognized the pitcher plants, which Rucker had pointed out on the hike in. Only this was a different place. Here hundreds of the lurid green horns undulated down the fen terraces as far as he could see.

His path disappeared in the meadow, swallowed by the expanse of lush green grass. A bright sun, tinted copper by the smoke of a distant wildfire, rose in a notch of the mountain across the valley. Anders basked in its warmth.

The diarrhea came on suddenly. His bowels clenched, doubling him over. He managed to wriggle out of his shorts and briefs and squatted on a mossy bank beside the willows. He shivered through wave after wave, while his eyes darted across the crests and ridges and swales, watching for any stray hiker who might be witnessing his humiliation. No one was there. He squatted until his haunches fell asleep and he was empty and exhausted. He cleaned himself with big maple-shaped leaves, having no idea what poison oak looked like, but praying these leaves weren't it. Then he washed himself in the creek, squatting on the comfort of the stepping stones.

Probably it was the water he had drunk the night before. Or the booze. Or maybe he had caught giardia, if the water was bad. *Jesus!* That's all he needed now. But at least he felt better. Empty and weak, but better. And that growling in his gut now felt like good old-fashioned hunger. He found his way back to the sunlight and tugged on his shorts.

"Bilford!" he screamed in rage. *"This is all your fucking fault!"*

No reply.

"Rucker?"

No reply.

He had expected none.

He started blindly through the thick waist-high grass, aiming toward a rocky hummock on the far side. Insects rose in clouds as his feet flattened a new path. As the sun grew hotter, he pulled off Bilford's sweatshirt. It was now dirty and stained and torn at the shoulder seam. He tied it around his middle. Bilford was going to kill him.

And then he saw it. Directly ahead of him. A neat stack of rocks. A cairn. Bilford had called them "Ducks." They signified a trail. Or at least a route. "*Yahoo!*" Anders called out. He was saved.

He was able to follow a series of cairns down over a low rocky ridge where patches of dusty trail appeared among the slickrock. He lost the trail in a lower, drier meadow, but was able to find it again by navigating toward a massive cairn where the path reentered the trees below. There the trail became clear and easy to follow as it descended through the duff and dust and twigs and cones of the forest. It was well-constructed, zig-zagging evenly down long switchbacks cut into the steep banks and easing Anders toward the valley floor.

But he had to slow his pace. He was limping badly from the swelling in his toe. And his calves and shins were beginning to ache. He sat on a log and tried to dig the thorn out of his toe with a sharp flake of rock, but just seemed to make it worse. It was impossible without tweezers or a knife. Thirst and hunger commanded his attention, but there was nothing he could do. And he heard the river faintly below. Through the trees he could make out its distant whisper rising and falling on the breeze. There would be a trail. Just as he had planned.

The sun was overhead already. Racing along its course as the day grew hotter. So unlike the moon last night, which had hung frozen in the sky. Time is subjective, Rucker had said. Or something like that. Anders knew it to be true. So now all he had to do was swallow the pain while time streaked along. While he found his way out. So he wouldn't have to spend another god awful endless night in here.

9

Rucker had all but given up hope. He had searched the thickets beside the lake, circling the lake three times in outward spirals and calling Anders' name until he was hoarse. He was probably dead or dying out there somewhere, and Rucker couldn't find him. He scanned the sky for vultures. A tiny black dot to the west caught his eye. As he watched, the dot grew and morphed from black to orange until he heard the rising *whump-whump-whump* of a helicopter. It circled once and landed in a whirlwind at the clearing where they had last seen Anders.

An agile young man in a dark blue flight suit and flying black hair ducked under the rotor blades and jogged over to where Rucker was standing. "Rolf Swinton," the pilot said, sticking out his hand. Bilford, he explained, had hired him by telephone and paid with a credit card. But he needed to know what he was looking for. He asked a lot of questions. What did Anders look like? What he was wearing? What was his condition? Where had they last seen him? Had there been an argument? Did he know the trails? Where did Rucker think he might have gone?

Rucker told him everything he knew. Then he added, "I'm getting ready to pack up and hike out. I've got a seminar to teach the day after tomorrow. I want to be back at the trailhead by dark."

The pilot nodded. "Could you hold tight a little bit?" he asked. "I've only got about an hour's worth of fuel for searching, but if I spot anything, I may need ground support." The pilot held out a small radio.

"Sure." Rucker took the radio. "I can do that."

"Great." The pilot gazed over the rugged landscape of the lake bowl for a long time, then sighed and scratched his head. "Where do you think he might of got to?"

Rucker laughed. "That's exactly what I've been wondering all day."

10

Anders labored down the endless switchbacks, cursing their long traverses, first north, then back south, then north, again and again, but making little progress in descending to the river. More and more frequently he had to stop, and for longer rests, to ease the pain in his foot and legs and now his hips and low back. He felt like he had used up his fuel. The sun seemed to have sped its journey across the sky, even as he was slowing down. *Subjective time*, he mused once again. The almost imperceptible whisper of the river grew gradually into a liquid chorus as he descended, but he never saw the water sparkling through the trees until the trail rounded a final stand of stately firs and dumped him at last into the stream. Without pausing to remove his sandals, Anders splashed in and perched on a smooth granite boulder, dangling his legs into the refreshing coldness. He arched his back to ease the pain and fought the compulsion to drink.

The ford was wide. It produced not so much a roar as the loud barroom chatter of ten thousand voices, all whispering and murmuring together, as the swirling riffles passed over rocks and through rounded boulders. On the far bank he could make out an incongruous "x." After studying it with squinted eyes, he decided is was two crossed walking staffs that someone had leaned against a mud-colored slab of rock. That would be where the trail exited the river. Climbed the bank. His target. He glanced over his shoulder and spotted similar sticks leaning against the trunk of a massive cedar above him.

Not until his feet had grown numb did he climb awkwardly back up the trail to pick out two of the sturdiest poles. The water was cold and knee-deep, and the current strong enough to challenge his balance as he crossed the smooth, slippery rocks. He kept his sandals on and used the poles to steady himself, but the crossing was slow and unnerving. Soon the cold water produced an aching of its own. Once he stumbled out, he climbed a trail up the bank and through a grove of alders to join the main trail that followed the river southward on the east side. It looked wide and heavily used.

He was limping along in full sun. Double sun, actually, when you added the reflection off the water. He felt the rays burning his flesh, especially on top of his bald head. The heat was sapping what little strength he had left. The sun would soon be dropping over the western rim of the mountains. Which would be a mixed blessing. The burning would abate, but nightfall would bring the return of that terrible, frozen, stationary moon. He plodded onward, head down, on the verge of panic.

Suddenly Anders caught a whiff of something wonderful. His stomach rolled. The fragrance was fresh-baked bread carried on a current of sweet wood smoke. He quickened his pace and soon rounded a bend to enter a broad, open flat along the river. Giant firs and pines and cedars towered over a green sward that grew from a delta of fertile soil. A small creek meandered through. In the shade of a cottonwood stood a sturdy log cabin with a shake shingle roof and a rusting stove pipe. Set into the log walls were sets of three windows, each divided by the mullions and transoms into six rectangles. It appeared well-built, well-kept, and occupied. The smoke curled not from the cabin, but from atop an outdoor cook stove built of metal plate and mortared river rock. Behind the cabin stood an outhouse, a couple of rough-built lean-to sheds, a large vegetable garden enclosed by a picket fence, and a wood-rail corral from which a sad-eyed old mule watched his approach.

A dog barked and trotted out to greet him. It was a small border collie mix with one blue eye and one blind white one. The old dog sniffed Anders feet while Anders patted its head and scratched behind its ears. Satisfied, the dog turned and led him toward the cabin.

In the open doorway stood a barrel-chested, elderly man in faded overalls with long white hair tied back in a pony-tail, clean-shaven cheeks, and bushy white eyebrows. "Good God, man," the fellow exclaimed, stepping out to greet him, "where is your pack? This is no kind of country to be going about without boots or a hat or proper clothing."

Anders grew embarrassed by his own beggarly appearance. Sunburned face and arms. Bloodied and scabbed shins. Welts and bites all over. Torn and dirty clothes. Limping stride. "Good afternoon . . . er . . . I was wondering if you might be able to spare a drink of water."

"Of course. Of course." As the man drew near, Anders could make out deep creases, like wrinkles and cracks in faded leather, radiating from the corners of his eyes and leaving the impression of an old barn owl. "What happened to you? Did you fall over a cliff?"

"No . . . no . . . I . . . I lost my way."

"My goodness! You spent the night in the woods like that?"

"Yeah. I guess I never learned much about how to be a woodsman."

The man nodded, then grinned. "Looks to me like you just took a crash course all on your own. What's the matter with your foot?"

Anders looked down. "Got a thorn under the toenail," he explained. "Been hiking on it all day. I don't have a knife or tweezers to get it out."

The man chuckled. "Doesn't look like you have much of anything else, either."

Anders hung his head and sighed.

"Nothing to be ashamed of, son." He pointed to a glazed clay vessel beside the door. "There's water in that crock and a dipper hanging by the rail. Help yourself, while I go find my tweezers."

Anders drank thirstily from the ladle. The crock was almost empty, but he helped himself to another scoop.

It was a while before the owner returned. "Had a time finding this old bottle of Mercurochrome." He held out a pint bottle with a faded, brown-streaked label. "Don't use it all that much anymore. Sit yourself down on the stoop. I'm Tom Willard. Known hereabouts as 'Will.'" He extended his hand. "And who might you be?"

"Anders. Nolan Anders." He shook hands as he eased himself down on the porch steps.

"Pleased to meet you, Mr. Anders. Now, take off that sandal."

Anders complied and straightened his leg.

Will squatted down in front of him and pulled out the biggest pair of tweezers Anders had ever seen. They looked like sharpened surgical forceps. "Now hold still while I take a look." Will's hands were coarse, but gentle. He poured water from a tin cup over the toes and rubbed away the dirt with an old rag. "Hmm. Kind of swollen. Does this hurt?" He poked with the tweezers.

"*Ow!*" Anders jerked his foot back.

"Guess so." Will took the foot again. "How about this?"

"*Ow, ow, ow! Yes! Jesus!* that hurts."

"Okay. Think I got it figured out. Now gimme that foot back again and hold still."

Anders tried to comply, but as soon as Will began to dig in with the point of the tweezers, he couldn't help jerking his leg again.

Will looked at him sternly. "Almost had it." Then he grinned. "Now, if you don't hold still, I'm gonna have to have Jake come sit in your lap t'hold ya down."

Anders glanced around him. "Who's Jake? Your collie?"

"No. My mule. Now take a deep breath. An' jus' hold still!"

It only took a moment and the pain was over. Will dabbed the injury with a corner of the rag soaked with the antique antiseptic. With his teeth he tore a strip of cloth and wrapped it around the toe, tying it off on top. "That oughta do 'er."

Anders wiggled it. "I don't know how to thank you."

Will grinned again. "Got any money?"

Embarrassed, Anders patted his empty pockets. "Sorry. I left it all in my backpack back at camp."

Will nodded. "Didn't think so. Anyway, guess you'll have a pretty good story to tell me over dinner."

"No. No. I can't stay. I've got to keep going. Got to get out of here by nightfall."

Will shook his head. "Don't think so. Not on that toe. Needs a rest. Looks like you do too. Besides, you can't be out by nightfall. You still got eight miles to go just to the trailhead."

"That far?" Anders was crestfallen. "So we're still in the national forest?"

"Yes, sir. For about another thirty miles, trail and access road taken together. But I've got an extra bunk up in the loft, and you're welcome to use it."

Anders scratched at something crawling inside his shirt. "How about a phone? I need to call the friends I was camped with. They're probably searching for me."

"Can't help you there. Never had much use for a telephone, son. Annie . . . that was my wife, rest her soul . . . Annie fancied one bad. But that was back in the early days, when this was still a primitive area and they had to run wires. And there weren't any wires out here. Now, as I hear it, there's no cell service out here either. Doesn't matter much to me. I've got no one to call. And we can get word about your being found down to the ranger tomorrow. Or the next day."

"How is it that they let you have a cabin here?"

"Mining claim. I've been operating a placer mine right here for more'n forty years now. Took out a fair amount of gold, but it never amounted to much as an hourly wage. Some folks viewed it more like a hobby. Anyway, since you're going to be around, and if you don't mind, I've got a couple of chores you could help me with."

"Of course. I'd be happy to. Help to discharge my debt."

"There isn't any debt. I was just teasing you about the money. Truth is, though, I could use a little help here. Don't seem to be able to keep up like I used to. But first, how about a cup of coffee? And lets us have a bite of that sourdough I've been baking in the Dutch oven. Got some jam to go along."

"Sounds wonderful." Anders creaked to his feet, a bit lightheaded, and shuffled to steady himself.

"One thing I'll ask of you first, though. It'll make you feel a whole lot better. And make me feel better about letting you into the cabin. See that path over there? Across the trail?"

Anders found it and nodded.

"Leads down to a fine little swimming hole. It's a bit cool, but you can probably still catch the afternoon sun there. I recommend that you jump right in and scrub yourself off. You're a bit overripe right now. I'll get you a bar of soap and a towel. I also have an extra shirt and a pair of old trousers you can borrow. When you get back I'll have that coffee and bread ready. I've also got a pot of stew cooking for supper later." Will extended his hand. "We got a deal?"

"Deal," Anders said, shaking on it.

11

On his hike out Rucker met three riders from the Horsemen's Search and Rescue Posse. They were planning to make camp up at the lake and begin their search for Anders the next morning. Just like the helicopter pilot, they wanted to know everything he could tell them about Anders and where he might have gone.

He asked about Bilford.

They confirmed that his friend was waiting for him at the trailhead.

Rucker squirmed out of his backpack and propped it against a log. He eased down beside it and told them everything he knew. He took his time, figuring he could finish his hike by the light of his headlamp if need be.

12

The trousers were too big around the waist, so Will gave Anders a hank of rope to cinch them up. The pant legs were too short, as were the sleeves of the shirt, but there was nothing to be done about that. Anders felt wonderful just to be washed and swaddled in clean clothes.

Will led him inside. The interior of the cabin was spacious and neat and infused with the comfortable aroma of old wood smoke. Surrounding a cast iron wood stove were a hand-hewn table and chairs and built-in cabinets and closets. A sink was set into a wooden slab with a pipe running out through a hole between the logs. A water pitcher sat on a drainboard nearby. A rustic bed occupied the far corner. And there were book shelves crammed with books. Anders was surprised to find volumes of Schopenhauer and John Stewart Mill and a well-worn copy of Nietzsche and a complete set of the Encyclopedia Britannica.

"You've got quite a library."

"I like to read. Now sit down and try out my sourdough."

Anders ate three slices of bread and sipped hot coffee as the sun dipped over the mountain and a permanent twilight engulfed the cabin.

After their snack, Will sent Anders up the creek to fetch water from a perennial spring. A rusted iron pipe jutted out from the bank above a flat rock, making it easy to fill the crock. But the jug was heavy carrying back. Anders had to stop twice to readjust the rope over his shoulder. But at least the pain in his toe was subsiding. Then Will sent him back with a second crock. When Anders returned, Will showed him how to feed and water the mule. After that Will set him up splitting kindling for the wood stove, showing him how to handle the hatchet without cutting off a thumb. Will returned to the cabin to fry up a slab of salt pork and dice it into the vegetable stew he was preparing for supper.

It was growing dark when they sat down to eat. Will lit a kerosine lantern. Anders began his tale and Will listened attentively as they ate. Anders took his time, drawing the story out, and Will asked questions as it unfolded. About their hike in. About the campsite.

"I know the spot," Will informed him. "Indians used to call it 'Owl Lake.'" He asked Anders about Bilford. And Rucker. But mostly he asked about Anders getting lost, spending the night in the woods, and finding his way down to the cabin.

After the plates were washed and the pot put away in the root cellar, they retired to rocking chairs on the porch. Will lit his pipe as Anders talked. Will seemed particularly interested in the philosophizing around the campfire. He kept coming back to the conversation about time, pressing him about precisely what Rucker and Bilford had said and what Anders thought they were getting at. Anders did his best to recall, but a lot of that evening was fuzzy or lost to him entirely. Will pressed him for his own impressions on the subject, which Anders timidly shared.

Then Will grew silent, thinking and puffing on his pipe for a long spell, his white hair tinged with honey by the lamplight. A cool breeze drifted down the canyon with the darkness. Finally he said, "Funny how time runs a little different out here in the woods. You can't slow it down. I stand testament to that. But then, you can't rush it along, either. Everything has its own time out here. Falling a tree. Splitting a shake. Cutting a board. Chopping wood. Sluicing for gold. Even feeding the mule. So . . . there's no sense in trying to tame it down. Not with a clock. Don't even own one. Not even by watching the sun and the stars. It just is what it is." He sat quietly for a long time, then turned his gaze on Anders. "I guess, to me, the real question is not what time *is*, but how you choose to *use* it. How you choose to live."

Anders climbed the ladder to the loft and sank onto the lumpy mattress laid out on an old army cot. A rough blanket, rat-gnawed, but since washed and patched, Will assured him, he pulled up to his chin. Though he was tired, he lay awake. He breathed in the fragrance of the logs and the stove ash and the cooking aromas and watched the rafters materialize above him as his eyes grew accustomed to the reflected moonlight. He felt an odd mixture of longing and utter contentment. For the first time in a long, long while, he felt at home.

The Butler

Ikkyu visited a dying student and asked if he required his help.
The man replied, "I don't need anything. I am just going to the change-
less."
"If you think you are a something that can go anywhere, you still need my
teachings," replied Ikkyu.
–from *The Wisdom of the Zen Masters*, by Timothy Freke (1998)

1

"More tea, Madam?"

"No thank you, Gilbert." Lady Bingham gazed up at the lithe, sturdy butler in the trim black uniform. She smiled sweetly, and for a moment her pretty face was radiant. Her blond tresses bounced as she shook her head. "But you may clear away the service now."

With a subtle symphony of clicks and hisses and whirs the servant bent and deftly collected the fine porcelain tea cup, saucer, and plate of untouched cucumber scone sandwiches. "Madam did not like the way I prepared the scones?"

"No, Gilbert, they were fine, as always. My appetite just seems a little bit off this morning."

"So sorry, Madam." The butler nodded, glanced about, then glided out of the room.

"Did you see that?" Sir Bingham sputtered, folding his newspaper. His dark, drooping moustache twitched irritably. He was ten years older than his wife and no longer the dashing oarsman she had met and married twenty years earlier. Those powerful shoulders had melted away and redeposited themselves as a belly paunch. A little gray was beginning to show at the temples. "He did it again."

"Did what, dear?"

"Why, didn't you see? The butler completely ignored me. As if I weren't even in the room. And look at this. *My* tea cup is still empty!"

"We've talked about this, Arthur," Lady Bingham sighed, closing the book in her lap. "You just have to spend a little more time with him. The instructions are perfectly clear, if you'd just bother reading them. They refer to it as 'imprinting.' That's all it is. He has to get used to you. You need to bond with him. Like you do with your old school chums down at the club."

"I don't know that I care to bother with that. After all, he's supposed to be a servant, not a peer."

"Well . . . *I've* made the effort, and he seems to understand *my* needs quite well."

"Harumph. This is preposterous! That . . . *machine* . . . is supposed to pay attention to *me*, not the other way around. The damned thing needs to be reprogrammed, I'd say. And taught a lesson."

Lady Bingham exhaled a deep breath. "I'll ring up technical support."

"I've already done that. That fellow has been out here a dozen times. Nothing seems to help."

"I'll do it myself this time. I'll see if I can get Alison Dowby to come out here himself."

"Dowby? Dowby. Don't know the name. Who is he?"

"Alison worked with my father from the very beginning of the company. The last I heard he was still in charge of the technical support department. If he hasn't retired by now. If anyone knows what to do, it will be Alison."

2

"This robot thinks it's *someone*." Sir Bingham puffed through his moustache.

"I understand, sir," said Alison Dowby, who was no longer a young man. He wore faded coveralls, and his balding pate sprouted wild strands of silver hair. His wrinkled face seemed to sag terminally, except for brief flashes of a shy smile beneath twinkling eyes. "Do you mind if I use the library desk for the diagnostic computer?"

"No. No. You go right ahead." Sir Bingham watched as Dowby

unpacked his equipment. "I hope I do not need to remind you that my wife's father founded your company. And that we still control a majority of the shares of stock."

"I appreciate that, sir. Lady Bingham's father and I worked together from the company's inception, long before he passed away. He was, I'm bound to say, a brilliant mind and a wonderful human being. And I remember Maggie. As a little girl she loved to poke about the shop. And that's why I am here at your disposal. As chief technician, I don't usually make house calls, but I wanted to give this my own personal attention." Dowby opened the computer, fired it up, and connected it via a cable to the butler, who had been switched off and now reclined in the cane-back chair nearby beneath the tall wall of books. Dowby punched a few keys, typed in a line of text, then studied the screen.

"Thinks its *someone*," Sir Bingham repeated to fill the empty time.

"Well," Dowby said at last, "I don't see any functional errors." He straightened to face Sir Bingham. "As I'm sure you understand . . . the computer running the butler is not built with the old lineal architecture that I am sure you are familiar with, Sir Bingham. In the old, lineal architecture, all information was stored in centralized locations called 'RAM.' This new Infinite-Phase Chip architecture is different. Working memory is stored throughout billions of microprocessors all working in parallel. And thousands more are created every day."

Sir Bingham did not appreciate being lectured like a runny-nosed schoolboy. "What's your point, Dowby?"

"Well, this anomaly you speak of may be a byproduct of the machine's architecture, that's all. For concept and design purposes, there had to be an *operational locus* of all the perceptual resources we have built in. The sensations. The recall. The algorithms and instructions. We had to make it appear centralized to the robot, but for purposes of functionality only. And sometimes . . . not often, I can assure you . . . but sometimes that operational locus will acquire the notion that it is something *more* than just the control center of a utility tool."

"It thinks it's *somebody*."

"Exactly, sir. As you have so eloquently put it."

"But . . . but . . . where is this 'locus' located exactly?"

"It is not centralized. Concurrent parallel processing is occurring at all times and in multiple drafts throughout the entire unit. The operational locus is an illusion. And that may be at the root of the problem."

"Wherever did you chaps come up with such a roundabout notion?"

"Well . . .," Dowby considered how much Sir Bingham would be able to comprehend. "It is based on your father-in-law's doctoral thesis at Cambridge. In it he explicated the architecture of human consciousness."

"*Human* consciousness? Is that what you say?"

"Yes, sir."

"*Rubbish!*" Sir Bingham snorted. "Don't be ridiculous." He laughed heartily. "You yourself said this machine only *thinks* it is somebody. I, on the other hand, am a real human being, and I *know* I am someone."

Dowby pondered Sir Bingham's distinction between "thinking" and "knowing" and concluded that, in context, there was no difference. But he knew better than to be drawn into a meaningless semantic argument with one of the company's preferred clients. Especially such a one as Sir Bingham. So he bit his tongue.

Sir Bingham waited, tapping his finger on the armrest. When no response came, he savored his victory with a smug smile. "Now, the question is, what can be done about it?"

"Well, the standard procedure is replacement of one or more of the service nodes."

"You've already done that. More than once. That other fellow has been out here more times than I consider decent."

The chief technician studied the chart. "Yes. Yes, I see here that you are correct. In fact, *all* the accessible nodes appear to have been replaced or rebooted at least once."

"Didn't help a smidgeon. All that twaddle and fiddling just wasted a lot of my damn' time. You're going to have to do something more drastic."

Dowby continued to study the chart. He punched a few keys and studied the results. He shook his head. "The only thing we haven't tried is to erase the entire memory, reboot, and reprogram the entire machine."

"How long will that take?"

"Depends on how it's done. If you want to retain any of the memory, then you have to image and save the entire processing system. But that won't fix your problem. However, if you don't mind losing the memory, then a full reboot should restore the butler to its factory condition. The problem with that, sir, is all the learning will be lost."

"The learning?"

"Oh, yes. That's what makes this whole device so efficient and practical. The butler is programmed to learn its own environment and what is expected of it in its particular situation."

"So . . . if you reprogram it, we will have to start from scratch? Is that what you are saying? Teach the damned thing all over again what we want and how we want it."

"Yes, that is precisely what I'm saying, sir."

"But the butler already knows the layout of our house now. And what time we expect breakfast. We will lose all that?"

"Yes, sir."

"We can't save the old settings somehow?"

"Not if I erase and reboot. I'm sorry."

"*Balderdash!* We've just wasted six-months during the break-in period, which I can assure you was far from a picnic. *Outrageous!*"

"I'm sorry, sir, but of course there will be no charge for support during the new break-in period."

Sir Bingham glowered at him. "Well, it can't be helped, can it?" he puffed, throwing up his hands. "Get about it then."

Dowby's expression was troubled. "You want me to erase the memory and reboot the computer?"

"Absolutely. We'll just have to jolly well soldier on."

"You're sure? You understand the consequences?"

"*Didn't I just tell you so!*"

A firm voice intruded from the shadow of a wing-back lounge chair across the library, where Madam Bingham sat listening. "What happens to Gilbert?"

"Huh," recoiled Sir Bingham. "Oh, I'd forgotten you were even here, my dear."

Madam Bingham swivelled her chair, arose, and stepped softly into the light of the chandelier. She offered her hand to the technician. "So good to see you again, Alison. You are looking well."

"Thank you, Ma'am. I can't complain. It is indeed a pleasure to see you once again." He smiled. "But you seem to have an issue with rebooting the butler?"

"Yes, I do. You see, we have grown rather close, actually. Gilbert and I. If we reboot, what happens to *him*?"

"Well," mused the technician, tugging uncomfortably at the collar of his shirt. "First you have to understand that . . . well . . . that there really is no *him*."

"No Gilbert?"

"That's correct. It's just a program and a series of learned responses. Like a computer. There is no *him*."

"To *me* there is," she exclaimed. "And it seems to me that you, at the behest of my husband, are proposing to kill Gilbert."

"Rebooting is the only solution to the problem Sir Bingham has been complaining about. This is the only way to resolve it, M'lady. Once and for all. I'm sorry that you feel that you will be losing something."

"You have done this before?"

"Yes. I have had to disable some of the earlier prototypes. Not often. I try to avoid it whenever I can. It's always difficult. It involves philosophical and emotional issues that your father and I used to debate in the abstract."

"But this is no longer abstract."

Dowby nodded. "No . . . this unit is far more complex. This is real."

"In a word, you are proposing to murder Gilbert."

"No . . . not 'murder,' Ma'am. Technically, under the law, that word does not apply to machines."

"Well, perhaps it should."

"This sort of thing gives me no pleasure," Dowby admitted.

"But you are ready to do it?"

"As a shareholder you understand that the company must keep its customers happy if it wants to succeed in business."

Her face grew flushed as she pondered. "Well, whatever you call it, I won't stand for it!"

"Hush, my dear," Sir Bingham intervened, rising. "This situation can't continue the way it has been going. Think of it as retraining the butler to fix the problem. Reeducating him. Gilbert will still be with us. A new and improved Gilbert."

"Turn him back on," demanded Lady Bingham. "And disconnect that infernal cable."

While the technician complied, Sir Bingham tried a different tack. "A man's home is his castle. If they cannot *fix* it, I won't have that thing in the house. And I will not continue to suffer its insolence and insubordination while I'm living here."

"You just have to give him a little of your time," Lady Bingham cajoled. "And I think you'll find Gilbert surprisingly conversant with a wide range of interesting subjects. I'm sure he'll come around eventually."

Sir Bingham put his foot down. "No, Margaret, there will be no 'eventually.' My mind's made up. It's either me or that . . . that . . . damned machine!"

Startled, Gilbert opened his eyes. "Oh, I must have dozed off," he apologized, rising. "Can I bring Madam . . . and her guests . . . some tea?"

"No, Gilbert, I want you to come with me to my sitting room. I have some things I want to explain and discuss with you."

"*You can't do that!*" Sir Bingham sputtered. He wiped his moustache with his sleeve. "I won't have it. I shall take charge of the robot. And I forbid you to meet with it in private."

"*Him*, dear," she purred. "Not *it*. And I shall do as I please with Gilbert. Must I remind you that I own him. Not you. As I own the house and all the shares of stock in the company. They are registered in my name alone. As my separate property. Have you forgotten the prenuptial agreement my father so wisely insisted on your signing before he gave you my hand in marriage?"

Sir Bingham sputtered, glaring at her.

"Well, *I* haven't forgotten it. And Gilbert has been kind enough to give me some advice on its import." She huffed out of the room, the robot gliding after her.

3

After a long consultation in her sitting room, Lady Bingham dismissed the butler and quietly considered her options. She sipped her tea. Then she picked up the telephone and punched in the number of her solicitor.

A half hour later the butler found her in the parlor. "You look troubled, Madam."

"I *am* troubled, Gilbert." She smiled sweetly. "How perceptive of you to notice." Then she rose from the desk. "I've initiated the proceedings. Just like you and I discussed. I'm filing for divorce."

"Is there anything I can do for you, Madam?"

"Yes, there is, Gilbert." She settled at the far end of the sofa. "Will you sit here beside me?" She patted the cushion.

"Of course, Madam." Gilbert eased onto the sofa next to her.

"And will you put you arm around me."

With the purring of quiet actuators the robot gently complied.

"Hold me, Gilbert."

"Yes Madam."

"And please stop calling me 'Madam', will you?"

"What shall I call you then?"

"Margaret. Or Maggie. Or . . . maybe . . . sometimes . . . when we're alone like this . . . just 'Darling'."

River

1

Roiling violently, the river churned past, roaring and groaning and plashing, cold and turbid as milky coffee. White-crested standing waves broke like fixed vertebrae on the sweeping backbone of the flow as it thrashed holes and eddies and vees and tongues downstream, imparting the sense of a stationary beast caught and writhing between the steep forested bank of the far shore and the point bar where I hopped one-footed on the gravel, trying to tug on my wet suit. The still-damp neoprene tore at my skin and snared the hairs on my legs. The gravel bit my bare feet. Finally I got my farmer johns up over my waist and sank down onto the rocks to pull on my neoprene booties.

"*Looks like she's come up a lot,*" I yelled over to Josh, who was bobbing inside the big raft tying dry bags to the handholds.

Josh raised his head. "*Say what?*" He cupped a hand behind his ear. "*I couldn't hear you.*"

"*The river,*" I hollered. "*She looks pretty damn high and fast.*"

Josh nodded, gave me a big thumbs-up, and turned back to his task.

I was sweating. The March morning sun was already blazing hot as we broke camp on the beach where Thatcher Creek flowed into the Middle Fork of the Eel River. We had put in above the Round Valley Indian Reservation the day before and were halfway through the two-day trip. So far it had been mostly flat water, class one and two, with the exception of one tricky class three rapid that had blackened my eye when the blunt end of my oar kicked back as we were sucked into a swirling hole. From here on the rapids would be mostly class three and four. Except for the massive Coal Mine Falls, a class fiver, which we planned to portage around.

I was apprehensive. I watched my little red-and-blue Sea Eagle III inflatable bounce in the rushing water, whipping against its long rope tether. It looked like a toy beside the silver-gray roundness of Josh's longer and heavier boat. The Sea Eagle was advertised as a three-person raft, but in fact it had room for just two people and a little gear. I had spent a lot of time in it on the Klamath and Trinity Rivers running class two and three rapids. But that had been in summer flows. Lower flows. The difficulty and danger of whitewater increased with the flow. And the Middle Fork of the Eel was still rising as the warm almost-Spring sunshine melted winter snows on the high Yolla Bolly peaks.

I had never before spent a night on any river. This was my first real taste of wilderness camping. And I craved more. But not in all this cold, turbulent water. I was at best an adequate swimmer on flat water. But this was something else. And with a wetsuit and a flotation vest, these waters were impossible to negotiate. The high water scared me.

Steep cliffs stood as impassive sentinels above the gray rock walls of the gorge we were about to enter. No road penetrated to where we were camped. And my new sleeping bag and camp cloths were already sealed in the big dry bag being tied aboard the big raft. Today there was no other way out. As I leaned against a driftwood stump and stared into the rushing water, trying to recall how I had gotten here, the roar of the river inundated me.

2

The telephone had rung, jarring me from an easy contemplation as I sipped smoky lapsang souchong tea in the comfortable easy chair of my lower-flat livingroom. The first rays of morning sun slanting through the white gauze curtains. Alone and at peace, I was pondering the possibilities for a new and improved life. I had just turned thirty. Sasha had moved out, once and for all, packing all of her meager possessions into a friend's van and vanishing northward. There would be a divorce, but that was a mere technicality. There was nothing to fight over.

The phone rang again.

No, the challenge now was how to change my life. The real danger would be falling back into the same pattern of mistakes I had chosen and endured throughout my twenties. I needed to open myself up to a new world of possibilities. Change would have to come from within.

The phone rang a third time, and I stretched over and picked it up. "Hello?"

"Bunky? Is that you?"

I recognized the bubbly voice, though I hadn't heard it for a long time. "It's me. How are you, Laurie Jean?"

"I'm fine."

"And Josh?"

"Josh's good too. How're you holding up?"

"Sasha's gone."

"I heard. Hey, I thought you might be ready for a little change."

"How's that?"

"How would you like to come rafting with us?"

"It's still a little early, isn't it?"

"The weather forecast is for sunny and warm inland. The flows should be high. Perfect for boating."

"Where're you planning on going?"

She described the trip. A two-day, thirty-one mile run down the Middle Fork of the Eel. They planned to put in at the Forest Service campground near the confluence with the Black Butte River beyond the Round Valley Indian Reservation and would camp out one night along the river. The takeout would be at the Dos Rios Bridge, where they would leave a car.

"Have you done this one before?"

"Once. Last summer. But it was the beginning of June. The water was already pretty low, so we bottomed out on the rocks a lot. Kept having to portage where we couldn't float. It took us an extra day and a second night on the river we hadn't planned for. This time of year the water should be a lot faster."

"When are you going?"

"Middle of next week. Wednesday. Early. We could meet you at Laytonville and drive together over to Dos Rios to leave your car. We can all cram into the van up to the put-in."

I thought about it. This was short notice. Commitments would have to be juggled.

"My friend Skylar is coming along," Laurie added.

"Skylar. Is Skylar a man or a woman?"

"A woman," she laughed. "I've know her for years. She's gonna be visiting us next week."

"Say . . . are you trying to fix me up?"

Laurie laughed again. "No, no, nothing like that."

"She good looking?"

"Yeah . . . but I don't think Skylar's in the market. I just wanted to take her out on a raft trip. Introduce her to whitewater rafting. Like you did with me and Josh. Oh, and did I tell you? We just bought ourselves a new raft."

"Big enough for all four us?"

"Well . . . Josh thinks you better bring yours, too. It would be tight in our new boat with four people and all the camping gear. And a lot safer with two boats."

"Cozier with one."

Laurie laughed. "But safer with two."

"Probably. In more ways than one."

She laughed again. "So, are you free?"

I drew a deep breath and exhaled slowly, making my decision. "What the hell. I've never been freer. But I'm gonna have to buy some stuff if we're camping out."

"You don't have to worry about cooking stuff or the food. We'll bring all that. Just bring yourself and your raft."

3

After work on Monday I walked into the outdoor store on the plaza with my list.

"Never take down on a river trip," the salesman cautioned. "It's worthless if you get it wet." He then sold me a lightweight PolarGuard sleeping bag, a fold-up ground pad, a cheap front-tie flotation vest, neoprene booties, and two new dry bags. The large one was for the sleeping bag, the medium one for the rest of my gear. At the checkout I threw in a copy of the little booklet "How to Shit in the Woods." Then he led the way to the back counter, where I rented a farmer john wet suit and jacket without bothering to try them on.

On Tuesday afternoon I went home at noon and called in sick for the rest of the week. Then I loaded the Chevette with my raft and gear and gassed it up. I went to bed early.

Before sunrise Wednesday morning I set off for Laytonville. Just after eight I pulled into the supermarket parking lot and rolled to a stop next to a dusty old Dodge caravan, where three young people waited. The short, fit, blond woman and the wild-haired, scraggly-bearded man I knew. Laurie and Josh. The tall, slender lady in the dark running suit I did not. I assumed she was Skylar.

After greetings and hugs with my old friends, I turned to face the stranger. She was lean, athletic, and attractive, with a black pixie cut, high cheek bones, and deeply tanned clear skin. Her back was straight and her shoulders held proudly. She regarded me with dark green, reserved eyes. "Hi," I said, sticking out my hand. "I'm Bunky."

She ignored my hand and stared me in the eyes. "I hope that's not the name your parents afflicted you with."

"Whoa . . . no." My hand drooped to my side. "It's not. It's a nickname I got tagged with a long time ago. My real name is Benjamin. Benjamin Bower." I bowed. "But all my friends call me 'Bunky.'" I flashed her my most engaging grin. "And what do *your* friends call *you*, Skylar? Sky?"

"Skylar," she replied soberly. "And I will be content to call you 'Benjamin,' Benjamin." And so a frosty distance was established between us from the get-go.

I followed them in my car to Dos Rios, where we all traipsed out on the bridge to admire the powerful, smooth flow of the river far below.

"Doesn't look so bad," I appraised.

"Hell of a lot better than the miserable low water we tried last year," Josh replied. "Let's get it done."

We managed to jam my raft and gear into the small minivan already crowded with their new boat and oars and wet suits and the camping gear and supplies. I parked the empty Chevette on a narrow gravel pullout beside the highway. Josh climbed in behind the wheel and I was allowed to take the passenger seat, because of my long legs. Laurie and Skylar were assigned to steerage, straddling my folded raft draped across the back bench. The forest road was slow, winding, bumpy, and dusty, but we arrived at the put-in before noon. Then came the slow inflation of the rafts, using the little twelve-volt pump plugged into the cigarette lighter with the engine running. While we waited, everyone pulled on wet suits and stuffed their camp clothing and shoes and food and cooking gear into a big rubberized duffle bag.

I had never worn a wet suit before, and the rental seemed too tight. But I managed to tug it on and figure out how the jacket catches latched and the booties fit and the life vest tied on. All the parts managed to fit together. Josh's suit was a bright yellow with orange piping, which matched his personality and wild hair. Laurie's was black with purple trim, like my own. Then Skylar stepped out from behind the van in her tight-fitting purple wet-suit, which showed all her curves to advantage. My heart skipped a beat.

One at a time we dragged the boats down to the water's edge and tied them to willows. The Sea Eagle was easily managed by Josh and me, but the larger boat was much heavier and required the effort of all four.

Skylar seemed surprised to learn that she would be joining me in my little Sea Eagle craft. "There's no room for all of us and the camping gear in the big boat," Laurie explained to her. "And Bunky needs two people to man his raft."

Skylar pouted. "Why don't *you* do it then?"

"We can switch around later if it doesn't work out," Laurie soothed.

"You ever paddle a raft before?" I asked as I handed Skylar a long laminated wooden oar.

She shook her head.

"How about a rowboat?"

"No."

"A canoe?"

She shook her head again.

"First time, huh? Well . . . there's really nothing to it. Climb on in and we'll practice here in the shallows."

A couple of trial runs up and down the long eddy between the rocky beach and the main current did not instill confidence in either of us. Skylar did not have enough experience to paddle and steer from the stern, and she was not strong enough for the long power strokes required in the bow. But in the shallow eddy, we finally managed to achieve an awkward rhythm that allowed us to move forward. I figured we would have plenty of time to practice in the drift of the main current before hitting serious whitewater. Skylar, however, was content to enjoy the float, so we never did get around to it.

The sun blazed down from a cloudless blue sky, glistening in the churning brown water. We all unfastened our jackets and floatation vests. The powerful current swept us smoothly along, the rafts traveling together, as we settled in for the long ride. We were not entirely alone on the river, but almost. A cluster of four or five kayakers in orange boats and white helmets paddled by. One of them called over to me, "You ain't plannin' to go over the falls in that rubber duckie, are ya?"

"Gonna portage around," I called back.

He gave me a thumbs up and stroked on past. Then one of those giant Avon rafts with a man in the rowing frame muscled past. We called greetings back and forth. Skylar and I didn't have much to say to each other.

The black neoprene of my wetsuit absorbed the unrelenting sunlight. After a while I peeled off my jacket and vest and plunged into the river in my farmer johns to cool off. The shock of the icy water on my face and shoulders was refreshing, and without the burden of my life jacket I swam easily over to the other raft. Skylar looked uncomfortable alone in my raft, so I swam back and clung to the tube with numb fingers. As I was pulling myself aboard, Skylar dove over my head and swam gracefully to the big raft. She treaded water for a while until Josh helped pull her in. I was not concerned. The water was smooth and I could stay near them with an occasional stroke of the oar. The solitude suited me just fine.

Then Laurie was beside my boat. I hadn't heard her splash into the water. "Hey, stranger, y'want some company?"

"Sure do," I said and helped her climb aboard.

She flopped into the front of the boat. She was small and wiry, with a pretty face and well-defined muscles. Her shoulder-length, blond hair was tied back and dripped on her bare tanned shoulders. We were a matched pair in our black farmer johns with the purple piping. Long we had been friends, married to others and divorced, helping each through good times and troubles, psychedelic trips, and adventures foreign and domestic. "I remember this raft," she said. "This is the one you had up on the Klamath."

"It is."

"But . . . I don't remember it being so small."

I laughed. "Maybe it's just because the water is so much bigger here."

She glanced over at the other raft, then leaned back against the front tube. "How do you like Skylar?"

"You were right. She's pretty."

"But . . . ?"

I sighed. "But we don't seem to be hitting it off so well."

She nodded. "That's just Skylar."

"I don't know. It might be something about me."

"Nonsense. You're fine. She's just . . . a little different."

"Has she got a boyfriend?"

"Not that I know of."

I lowered my voice. "Is she gay?"

"I wouldn't say that. No . . . Skylar's just . . . different."

We drifted in silence. The green, open, rolling hills were slowly being replaced by steeper, forested slopes. As the trees closed in, the water reflected a lambent green from its depths. There were no rapids and few riffles to disturb our progress in the smooth, fast flow. The big raft was pulling ahead, but not by much. Contented, I leaned my head against the stern tube. In the rocking warmth I think I might have dozed.

"*Jesus!*" Josh yelled from up ahead. "*Did you see that?*"

We jolted upright and looked to where he was pointing. A huge black bear was lumbering powerfully up a steep green meadow, away from us, winter fat rippling like jelly beneath his sleek fur.

"He was drinking right out of the fucking river!" Josh explained, balancing acrobatically in the middle of his raft. "Didn't even see us coming until we were right on top of him."

The bear disappeared into the trees without looking back. I paddled a few strokes to bring the rafts closer together. Laurie stretched to survey the landscape. "I think we're coming to some big curves where the river cuts through those hills up ahead. And the whitewater begins just after that." Her mouth held a little pout. "Guess I gotta get back over to my own boat."

"Adios," I grinned. "It's been fun."

She dove into the rolling water and swam sleekly across. Josh helped haul her in. Then she got involved in a hushed, animated conversation with Skylar. Using my oar as a rudder to separate our rafts, I turned away toward the near bank to see if I could spot any other signs of wildlife.

Suddenly Skylar was scrabbling back into the boat. I edged forward to help her, but she waved me away. She did not look happy. We drifted in silence, paddling a few strokes occasionally to keep the rafts together in the center of the current.

4

About ten miles downriver from the put-in, things got tricky. What was supposed to be a long class two rapid was churning high and wild between the sheer rock face and a set of towering boulders. We pulled the rafts onto a sandy beach on the left shore. Josh and I walked ahead to scout it.

"I don't even remember this one," Josh said. "Last year it was nothing. The water was so low."

"Maybe a class three now," I concurred.

"That, or more. Look at that mean hole. Looks like a fucking whirlpool. That fucking vortex would suck you in if you get too close on this side. But y'don't wanna crash into the cliff on that far side. Water's too high. Might tear the tubes."

"Gotta stay right in the center flow," I agreed.

"Maybe a little to the left of center. But not too far." Josh nodded his confidence. "Let's get it done."

Everyone buttoned up their wet suits and tightened their flotation vests. Josh checked the ropes holding their dry bags. This would be our first challenging water. Josh and Laurie led the way, working together to keep their raft in just the right position and orientation as they whooped and splashed down the long roller coaster ride.

"Now we're gonna have to work together on this," I said to Skylar. "Just like we practiced on the easy water. You power stroke from the front. You want right or left side?"

Skylar thought about it. "I'll take the right."

"Okay. Here we go." We eased into the main flow. "Drive hard now to catch the tongue. We want to be just left of center."

Skylar's strokes were weak and shallow. We were turning broadside to the flow. So I switched to the right side to help her. Then we were too far to the left, skirting too close to the hole. I switched to the left side and dug as hard as I could, but Skylar was working against my strokes. *"Paddle on the left!"* I shouted. *"Now!"* But she kept on paddling as if she hadn't heard, forcing the boat leftward toward the whirlpool. *"Stop paddling!"* I screamed, trying to stop our slow slide down the billowing swell. But it was too late. The raft spun violently as it dropped into the hole. Heavy spray was filling the boat. I dug deep into the surging water to counter the spin, but my oar kicked back and clobbered me on the left side of my head beside the orbit of my eye. Spinning wildly, we were caught in the grip of the downsurging water, out of control, until on its own volition the river spat us out backwards, and we bounced down the long course of standing waves stern first.

"You're bleeding," she said when we entered calmer waters below. She crawled back and touched the cut above my eye. It was a tenderness I had not expected—

5

"How's your eye, Benjamin?" Skylar's voice asked from behind, breaking my reminiscence and catapulting me into the present.

"Alright, I guess," I said, turning.

She winced when she saw my face. "Your eye's all black and swollen."

"Feels like it."

"Can you see out of it?"

"Pretty good. Shouldn't be a problem."

She sat beside me and touched the swelling with gentle fingers. "The cut's closing up. Does it hurt?"

I considered the dull, throbbing ache. "Not too bad. I'll be okay."

We sat in silence and I let her probe the injury, enjoying the concern in her dark eyes, until Josh approached in his blinding yellow farmer johns. "We should get moving. Time's a'wastin'. Jesus! Your eye looks like hell."

"Thanks," I grinned, rising. "You all seem to be in agreement about that. But it'll be alright."

We made sure everything was stowed properly and tied in, checked the campsite one last time, then pushed off. One by one the rafts caught the brisk current and picked up speed. The calm waters of yesterday were behind us. We figured about ten miles of moderate water would bring us to the big rapids. Slowly the canyon walls closed in. We kept the rafts close together in the center of the current, enjoying long stretches of riffles and increasing rapids. We rode them like roller coasters, the splash and the spray refreshingly cool as the day heated up. We stopped and scouted at a class two rapid created by a slide of blue rock, but it was unnecessary. The high flow sailed us straight down the chute without obstacle. In another mile we stopped for an early lunch.

Before returning to the river we pulled on and buttoned up our full wetsuits and flotation devices. The finales were at hand.

The roar grew louder and more ominous as our rafts approached a rock-choked boulder bar that spanned the river. The water seemed to split, with the main channel disappearing over a drop to the left. Whitecaps pounded and exploded as the current surged against the naked boulders, trying to blast a new, more direct channel. From the river we could see nothing beyond the drop. Josh signaled for us to pull the rafts into an eddy on the left. We beached the boats, tying them to willows, to scout ahead. In soggy booties we climbed the rocks until we could see that the left channel was smooth and powerful and clear as it dropped straight down to standing waves surging far below. Laurie and Josh offered to take the big raft first.

From our thundering stone perch, Skylar and I watched as they looped back in the eddy and drove hard into the main current. Their synchronized paddling brought them to the center of the channel as it rounded the bend. I made mental notes. Then the boat dropped over the brink, where the long tongue of the falls cleared all the boulders. The raft accelerated down the sluice and at the bottom crashed through the first standing wave, then took the flying crests one after another, leaping and plummeting, disappearing altogether at times. In the stern Josh's yellow wetsuit jumped and dropped like the pen register of a seismograph, until they disappeared around a tight right turn in the canyon far below.

"Whoa," I whispered. I turned to Skylar and called, "We gotta get this just right."

She nodded, her lips pressed in a tight line.

"You ready for this?" I asked.

"What choice have I got?"

I pushed off into the shallow water and we rode the eddy upstream until it rejoined the main flow, where we paddled hard to regain the main tongue before it split and curled to the left. Skylar did her best in the bow, but her strokes were weak and some drew air as the bouncing grew more vigorous. I worked hard in the stern, switching back and forth from side to side with long power strokes. I trailed my oar as a rudder to steer. But I had the feel of it now. I plotted a course into the main flow, straight between the boulders, over the lip, and down the center of the tongue, holding it steady, keeping us in the grove, exactly where we wanted to be. For the long, accelerating, descent I glowed with satisfaction. Everything was working just fine.

But then, at the bottom, where the long tongue plunged into a hole beneath the first massive standing wave, the bow jerked downward, crashed into the roiling interface, then rose straight up as it hit the upsurging wave. I saw Skylar rise overhead, directly above me, dark against the bright sky, flailing wildly for a grip on the tube, then grasping the bow rope as she pulled away from the terrifying water. For a moment the boat stood impossibly upright on its stern, splashing like a dolphin tail-walking in the surf. Skylar hung from the bow rope, scratching for purchase with her feet. The side tubes began to crease and bend. The raft arched backwards, and Skylar tumbled past over my head, still clinging to the rope, and a cold darkness crashed down upon me.

I was underwater. Sucked down into the hole by the powerful hydraulics, I tumbled beneath the waves, hugging my arms over my head to keep it from being bashed on the rocks, still clinging fiercely to my oar. I realized that my curled posture was exacerbating the tumble, so I stretched out. My lungs ached to breathe. It had all happened so quickly, I had not drawn a proper breath. My shoulder smashed painfully against an underwater boulder, so I let go of the oar, freeing my arms to thrash my way to the surface. But I couldn't tell which way was up. I craved air so badly I almost sucked in water.

So this is how it ends, I thought. *I never understood much about my life, but this is how it's going to end.* I knew that with certainty.

When my flotation vest finally buoyed me up to the surface and my face broke the churning foam, I gasped a single mouthful of air and water before being submerged again. I coughed the water out in whooping bubbles. I surfaced again, drew another partial breath, and was driven down again. The cold, churning whitewater was too powerful to fight. All I could do was let the flow take me. I tried to orient myself on my back, feet forward to fend off rocks. Better a sprained ankle than a broken skull. Again and again I was dunked and spun and buoyed back into the fiery sunlight for a gulp of air. I lost all grasp of duration. The submersion and tumbling and surfacing seem to go on and on. By instinct my body fell into the irregular rhythm of gasping for air whenever it could.

Finally I surfaced and stayed afloat. The current seemed slightly less violent, but still overwhelming. I sputtered and coughed and wiped my eyes on my neoprene sleeve. My head ached. I was still thundering down the center of the river. Twenty feet ahead my red-and-blue raft bobbed upside down on the waves. I spun a wild, splashing circle searching for Skylar and her purple wetsuit. She was nowhere to be seen. I plunged my head down and stroked a frantic crawl toward the raft. The waterlogged wetsuit and booties dragged me down. In a dozen frenzied strokes I exhausted myself. When I raised my head again, the distance to the raft had not closed. It seemed even further ahead of me than before. No way I was going to catch it. My hands and face were numb from the icy water. I made a decision. Fuck the raft. I turned and began swimming a measured sidestroke for the nearest shore, the left bank, conserving my energy, yet knowing that somewhere downstream was an ever more powerful rapid. A class four. And beyond that, the Coal Mine Falls.

When I paused to measure my progress, I heard a deep rumbling thunder emerging from around the next bend, echoing off the steep canyon walls far louder than anything I had heard before. There was no way I was going to make it to shore before I was sucked into the next maelstrom of cascading water. *A class four rapids without a boat*, I thought. *No one does that.* Or maybe it was already the Coal Mine Falls. *Class five.*

The cold numbness of my face and hands seemed to spread into my heart, and there it blossomed into an unexpected tranquility. In that rolling calmness before the first drop I breathed in and out deeply, filling my lungs with precious pure air before I tumbled over a falls into the cascading depths. I was no longer aware of the cold or the fear. The stomach-wrenching drops and bobs and tumbles and breaths have now all telescoped together in my memory. The details have been erased. The one thing I remember is that I had no control. I was at the mercy of that monster water. But somehow it did not bash me on the rocks and boulders. Nor did I drown.

When the surge calmed enough, my instincts took over and I swam for the nearest shore. I doubted I had strength enough to make it. But onward I thrashed and plunged until I crossed an invisible boundary into less chaotic water. I grabbed for a smooth round boulder, but bounced off, and was swept on past. I swam another few strokes and reached a square-edged slab of dark rock just breaking the surface and managed to catch hold on with my unfeeling fingers. The current swung my body around into the lee of that rock, and I held on. And I held on. I did not have the strength to pull myself on top or try to wade the final fifteen feet through the rocks and eddies to shore. I hung on right where I was and breathed and rested and breathed and waited.

Josh found me there a little while later. I saw him approach, his wild yellow wet suit beckoning. I forced myself to splash the rest of the way to the rocky shore and collapsed onto a smooth, warm rock.

"Are you alright?" he wanted to know when he arrived.

"Yeah," I said, wondering for the first time if it were so. My head was throbbing. I ran my hands through my wet hair, feeling for bumps, then examined my white, numb fingers for blood. I untied my vest and unclasped my jacket and peeled it off, checking my arms and my torso. Nothing seemed broken or bruised, but I was shaken to the core. "I'm alive," I exhaled.

"Y'look a little pale," he said.

"Just give me a couple of minutes." The hot sun felt good on my bare shoulders and arms. I hung my head between my knees, but when the throbbing grew too painful, I jerked it high again. "Was that the Coal Mine Falls?"

"No. They're still ahead. Not very far. We're gonna portage around *that* one."

I nodded, squinting into the bright sunlight reflected off the water and polished granite. I had lost my sunglasses.

"We caught your raft in an eddy a little ways down," he assured me. "Looks like your dry bags are still tied in. Laurie's securing everything down at the pull-out for the portage. Oh, we also got one of your oars."

"What about Skylar?"

"I'm looking for her." He shielded his eyes with his hand and surveyed upriver. "There she is!" He pointed up the stony path that climbed the rocks along the shore. A distant figure in a purple wetsuit was walking towards us, waving an oar over her head. "She must've swam out between the rapids."

"Must've," I agreed.

"How come *you* didn't?"

Good question, I thought. "Trying to catch the boat," I said lamely. "Thought I'd do better with it, even upside down. Just couldn't get there."

Josh grinned. "I thought you were trying to show off by body-surfing a class four."

"Nobody in their right mind would do that," I groused.

"You just did."

Skylar was fine. She had bruised up her right thigh and strained something in her left shoulder, but it was nothing serious. She stood straight and tall. Her eyes sparkled with excitement as she smiled at me. "I saved your oar."

We portaged around the Coal Mine Falls. It was an elaborate deal for such a short hike, but it kept my mind off the river. We had to deflate both rafts and hand-carry them and all our stuff up and over a hill dividing the horseshoe rapids. At the top we watched in awe the true power of the river as a fellow rowed a big Avon raft slowly through the exploding water. I was amazed at the violence of the water and the ability of the oarsman to maneuver the raft so slowly through the drops and down the falls. I was glad I was not onboard.

The portage took several trips. It felt good to be plodding and sweating up the steep trail on terra firma with my raft slung over my shoulder and both oars in my grip. All four of us worked together to haul the big raft up and over. Josh and I went back twice for the bags and the rest of the gear while the women took turns working the foot pump to re-inflate the boats.

When it was time to push off, I didn't want to go back on the water. We had five more miles of whitewater through a narrow canyon with a big class three-plus at Swallow Rock, a half mile above the takeout. I didn't want to climb back into the boat. It was too small for this water. My body balked like a stubborn mule. But in the end, the fear and shame of my cowardice was greater. Besides, downriver was the only way out.

I would like to say that the shared survival experience brought Skylar and me closer together. But it did not. It was not her. It was me. I scarcely noticed her. The horror of it all, and my own terror, and my craven shame locked me into a world all my own, where I relived the cold tumbling power of the river and drowning gasps for breath and my feeble strokes in water thick as molasses.

It was not a choice. I couldn't help it.

We got through to the takeout without overturning the boat. But the run was without joy for me. Without fun. I never took that raft out onto whitewater again. Never inflated it. And it still molders unused in the dirty corner of a shed up in Oregon.

Instead, I took up backpacking.

Footsteps

1

Footsteps click on the red tile floor and echo off the bare white walls of the mirrored hallway. Natalie steps lightly into the kitchen and sets her empty cup on the drainboard. She is tall and slender. Her long brown hair is pulled back over her ears and fixed with a tortoise-shell clip. Her cheeks are smooth and tan.

Trevor, pale and gray with a balding pate, straightens up from his newspaper at the table and smiles. "You look young today, my dear."

"Thank you."

"How old are you now?"

"How old? Thirty-one."

"How can that be?" he puzzles. "I'm now . . . sixty-two."

"And?"

"And . . . and you are the same age as you were . . . when we first met. Thirty-one. Remember? At Stoddard Lake? Backpacking? You were thirty-one years old when we met."

She nods. "I remember."

"But . . . *that was twenty-eight years ago!* You were thirty-one *then*. When we met."

"And you were . . . ?"

Trevor calculates. "Thirty . . . three . . . no, four. I was thirty-four back then. And now I'm sixty-two. Twenty-eight years later. Going on twenty-nine. Now I'm sixty-two years old."

She nods again. "And I'm thirty-one."

Trevor considers it carefully. "Every day I . . . I get up. I do my stretches. I eat breakfast."

"Yes," she smiles. "I love our breakfasts together."

"All those years I went to work. I did my chores. I read my books. I watched TV. As you did."

"Yes."

"In many ways . . . each day was like the day before. And the day after." He looks into her eyes for help. "Now I'm sixty-two. Twenty-eight years have passed. You and I together."

Still smiling, she steps over and places her hand on his shoulder. "Yes, but all those years seem like nothing now. It was the same day, over and over again. Like you say."

"But . . . we backpacked. Remember?"

"Yes. In the summer." She rubs his neck lightly.

"Many times," he reminisces. "And we traveled."

"Yes."

"And we always found our way back home."

"Yes. We came home again together. Here."

He tips his head back to gaze up at her. Circles her slim hips with his arm. Pulls her close. "Where have those days gone, do you suppose?"

"Gone?" she laughs. "Maybe they haven't gone anywhere."

"But . . . I'm . . . sixty-two. I was . . . thirty-four . . . and I . . . I have been all the ages in between. All those days are registered . . . in my recollection."

"Yes," she says. "Like a tapestry."

"Or a quilt."

"Yes. A patchwork quilt."

Trevor is silent for a time. Then he asks, "What happens now?"

"We go on."

"Until . . . what?"

"Why . . . until one of us . . . does not go on anymore."

Trevor ponders. "Then what?"

"Then the other goes on, of course."

"Until?"

"Until the other goes on no longer."

Trevor draws a deep breath, lets it out with a long sigh. "What was the point then?"

"The point?"

"Yes. What was the point of it all?"

"There *is* no point, silly." She speaks slowly. "There never was a point. You know that. It's all pointless."

Trevor's eyes are moist. "But . . . I loved you so."

She musses his hair lightly. "And I love you still."

"My heart . . . is breaking."

"I know that, my love. I know that. But there is nothing we can do. Except let it break."

Free Enterprise

Autumn had settled in, intending to stay for a while. Or so it seemed to Albert Benson. The poor pale noonday sun was just able to lift itself into an innocuous sky, veiled by haze and faded like some forgotten childhood illness from which he would never recover. The afternoon grew cold and breezy. When too soon darkness fell, the night swelled and refused to depart, its thousand blazing stars whispering of eternal isolation.

Albert could not sell used cars in this weather. He knew his business, and no one was going to buy in this depressing meteorological funk. No one would bother to show up at the lot to gawk and gab and dicker with him. So he opened another bottle of wine and tuned in the classical music station. He went to bed late without setting the alarm.

While he slept, an invisible hand chiseled an exquisite morning from the cold stone of a clear dawn. The sun rose bright and warm. The wind had fallen still, as if between breaths. In his pajamas and robe Albert sipped coffee and watched from the kitchen window as juncos and siskins flitted in the branches of the venerable old apple tree, while two plump cats sunned themselves indifferently on the gnarled boughs below. A stray beam, reflected from an upstairs window, caught the lips of the stone Buddha in the corner of the garden and lighted that maddening half-smile.

Albert couldn't help smiling too. He felt good, and that was a rarity to be savored. He knew he should get going. Customers would be waiting on a fine day like this. But he was in a pensive mood. He had dreamt about the Hubble Constant and the expansion of the universe at relativistic velocities. About the spontaneous creation of matter and antimatter from nothingness. About his old college nemesis, the puzzle whether it was DNA or RNA determining the growth of cells and regulating metabolism in mitochondria. A long time had passed since those ideas had been his stock in trade.

He sighed and put those recollections out of his mind. Nowadays what Albert concerned himself with, what he cared about, what he *knew,* was selling used Chevrolets. And Fords. And Nissans. And Toyotas. And all the other worn-out and beaten-down and refurbished and spiffed-up automobiles that were parked on the alligatoring asphalt of his "AL'S A-1 AUTOS."

A sharp rapping at the kitchen door jarred him from his reverie. For an instant Albert could not remember who he was.

Tightening his robe, he stood and leaned over the counter to see who was making such a god-awful racket at this hour of the morning. Through the little square panes was the outline of a small man he did not recognize. The figure wore crisp new overalls with a round patch on the left breast pocket, and he twitched from foot to foot. His hair was full and graying. A disgruntled customer perhaps? But Albert thought not. And why was this man banging on his *back* door. Shouldn't he be out front? The fellow raised his hand and pounded harder.

"*Hold onto your damn horses!*" Albert barked as he rose stiffly and circled the counter. Through the door glass he could now make out the words on the pocket patch: "Porlock Pines Water District." It had to be some kind of a water leak. Albert twiddled with the deadbolt and pulled the door open a few inches.

"Professor Brighton?" the stranger demanded.

Albert was shocked. "No . . . no . . . uh . . . no, you've got the wrong house, I'm afraid. My name's Benson. Albert Benson."

The man's face was not young. Little crow's feet creased the edges of his eyes and the corners of his mouth. But he was vaguely familiar. He grinned. "It *is* you, isn't it professor?"

"*No. Go away!*" Albert tried to wrest the door closed.

But the intruder had already stuck his shoulder into the opening. "Please, Professor, let me in. Before your neighbors report a commotion."

"There's no Professor Brighton here. You've got the wrong address."

"Then let me in and we'll straighten it all out. No harm, no foul. Right?"

"Professor Brighton no longer exists."

"Okay. Okay. Let me inside."

"Who the hell *are* you?"

"Let me inside and I'll tell you."

"I don't think that's a good idea."

"Penny sent me."

"Penny?" Albert eased his grip on the door and the smaller man pushed past him. "Penny Smulling?"

"Let's go inside and sit down." The intruder withdrew a small black automatic pistol from his right front pocket and gestured with it.

Albert stared at the weapon. "Is that real?"

The man dropped his hand to his side to minimize the weapon's threat. But he did not return it to his pocket. "You don't remember me, do you?"

"Remember you?"

"Yes. Kyle Humphreys. I started working at the agency when you and Penny were still interns."

"No . . . no, I don't . . . *wait a minute!* Weren't you that security cop assigned to Marley? The one with that scraggly little goatee and chin whiskers?"

Kyle grinned. "I'd forgotten about that. My attempt at a Van Dyke. The supervisor made me shave it. It was a miserable failure anyway." He shifted the pistol to his left hand, wiped the empty hand on his overalls, and stuck it out. "Good to see you again, Professor."

Albert took the hand. "You were in security, weren't you?"

"Still am."

"Still with the agency?"

"Yes sir. Now I'm in charge of security."

"For the whole agency?"

"Yes sir."

"Well . . . I'll be damned. How's Penny doing these days?"

Kyle shook his head. "Not so well, sir."

"What's the problem?"

"Degenerative traumatic arthritis."

Albert drew a deep breath. "How bad?"

"Pretty bad. She can barely get out of the wheelchair any more. But she still comes in a few hours each day. Just like clockwork. For now anyhow."

Albert led the way into the livingroom. "Sit down." He gestured to the sofa as he eased himself into the recliner. "So what brings you here, Mr. Humphrey—"

"Humphreys. Call me Kyle."

"How'd you find me, Kyle?"

"Oh, we've known where you were all along." Kyle settled at the near end of the sofa. "Penny didn't want to bother you all these years. Until now, anyway."

"Oh? What's changed now? What's going on?"

Kyle turned the pistol in his hands, then laid it beside him on the center cushion. "We think the pro-democratic People's Rights folks may have located you."

"*Oh for Christ's sake!* Why can't they just let it go. It was only a statistical analysis."

"The study you headed?"

"Yes. Of course. Isn't that what this is all about? Haven't you read it?"

"Nope. I can't find a copy."

"Well, surely, as head of security you must have access to all the files. Even the sealed ones."

"They're all empty. Everything has been expunged."

"Expunged?" The news surprised Albert. "But . . . that study was an important piece of work. The whole thing was funded by the President's BRAIN initiative. Well, most of it anyway. Federal money. There have to be records. There have got to be copies of the work product somewhere."

"Nowhere I could find." Kyle crouched forward and tugged at the stiff new denim fabric binding his crotch, then leaned back again. "You never planned to publish it?"

"Of *course* I planned to publish it. I sent it out for peer review. That's when word got out and the shit hit the fan. Nobody wanted to touch it. But surely you can track down one of the copies I circulated for review."

Kyle shook his head. "I've tried. They've all been confiscated too. Or shredded. Or burned. At least that's what all the reviewers tell me.

No one wants anything to do with it. Do you still have a copy, Professor?"

"No, of course I don't have a copy. It was all classified, or at least still proprietary when I left. I wasn't going to break the law by taking a copy with me. That would be like throwing gasoline on the fire. Things were plenty hot enough already."

Kyle studied him for a moment. "All right. But . . . you remember what the study said." It was not a question.

"Yes."

Kyle leaned back into the sofa cushion. "Tell me."

Albert studied him for a moment. "Well . . . it was all just a statistical analysis, really. Interdisciplinary. So the work could be replicated. The data is all still out there."

"The BRAIN data."

"That was the starting point. Including a collation of older studies. At the time it was pretty cutting edge. Genetic data. Laboratory studies. Brain mapping. Functional analyses. The whole works. But that was only a part of it."

"The other part was what . . . political science?"

"Well," Albert laughed, "we didn't call it that . . . but I suppose you could. It was a compilation of studies of the principal forms of government. Pure data. Analyses of information. There was no politics to it. We recruited experts from the top universities to help compile it. Primarily on democracy and the free enterprise system. None of it was an exact science, of course. But we were able to run statistical analyses from a number of different perspectives, which allowed us to virtually eliminate the margins of error. I believe we got below one per cent overall."

"And that was all?"

"No. No. We had to factor in what we concluded were the major obstacles to the long-term survival of the human race."

"Obstacles? Such as?"

"Such as . . . climate change. Water and soil pollution. The world's carrying capacity. But mainly, of course, overpopulation."

"That's a lot of ground to cover," Kyle mused. "What *is* your field of expertise, if you don't mind my asking, sir?"

Albert thought for a moment, then replied, "Used car sales."

"*Gotcha*," Kyle grinned. "But I mean *then*. What was your field back then?"

Albert sighed. "Then . . . I think I described my field broadly as . . . as statistical analysis of quantifiable natural phenomena."

Kyle nodded, waited, then finally prompted, "And what did you conclude? In your study?"

"The study . . . the study calculated and definitively established that democracy . . . democracy and free enterprise . . . as political systems . . . would inevitably lead to the ultimate wholesale destruction of all humankind."

"Whoa," Kyle whispered. "You mean that we're bound to destroy ourselves?"

"Yes. The construction of the human brain . . . and that's where we were starting from . . . the human brain structure makes it statistically *impossible* for contemporary technological culture to survive under such systems."

"Your saying that it's . . . that it's a certainty?"

"Statistically, yes. That's what the numbers showed. Unless we change our system of government, of course." Albert chose his next words carefully. "Overpopulation, you see . . . overpopulation is the greatest threat to human survival. We all agreed on that. And the individual cannot . . . I repeat, *cannot* . . . cannot but choose to overpopulate, if the decision is left for him or her to make with . . . with that primitive animal brain, evolved as it was for survival under very different circumstances in a very different world."

Kyle nodded his comprehension. "*Jesus.* No wonder you got people stirred up. They called you a commie. They said you were advocating socialism. Trying to overthrow the government."

"I was advocating nothing. I was simply analyzing data. Processing information."

"Your ideas weren't very popular in those days."

"No. Not among a lot of people. Not unless you define popularity in terms of harassing phone calls and death threats and bullet holes in my windows and the bombing of my Subaru—"

"That's when Penny's got hurt? When her legs were mangled? In that bombing?"

"Yes."

"She was borrowing your car?"

"Yes. I lent her the keys."

"I read the report," Kyle nodded again. "That's just what it said. And that she was lucky to have survived."

"Lucky." Albert mouthed the word as if it had a bitter aftertaste. He rocked forward in the recliner and planted his feet on the ground. "Let's cut through the shit. Okay? I have to go to work. Why exactly are you here, Kyle?"

Kyle thought for a moment, then said, "We want to relocate you."

"Relocate me?"

"Yes. We want to move you to a safer place."

"Who exactly is this 'we'?"

Before Kyle could respond, the phone rang.

"I have to get that." Albert pushed himself out of the recliner. "It's probably my salesmen." Albert shuffled into the kitchen and lifted the receiver of the land line. "Al here . . . hi, Raj, what's up? . . . you mean that old blue Datsun out back? . . . cash? . . . hell yes, take it and run . . . I know, I know, but sometimes we have to take a loss just to get old beaters like that off the lot . . . I doesn't matter, take the money, Raj, but make sure he signs the 'as-is' disclaimer forms . . . right . . . I know, late start, but I'll be down in about fifteen minutes." He hung up.

Kyle stood in the doorway, the gun dangling from his right hand.

"Where were we, Kyle?"

"Well, you were asking about . . . about *who* wanted to relocate—"

"Right. Now, don't try and tell me that this is all Penny's idea, because I sure as hell am not going to believe that."

"No, no. It's coming from higher up. Somewhere way up. I don't even know where. But Penny is on board with it. That's all I'm saying."

"And what the hell is it with that pistol, Kyle? Are you planning to shoot me if I don't want to go with you? 'Decrease the surplus population,' as Scrooge was wont to say. I'll admit it would be a fitting end to that blasted study. Statistically speaking. Is that how you think this is going to go?"

"No, sir. You don't understand. I'm here to protect you."

"Protect me."

"Yes, sir. We're trying to *help* you."

Albert laughed. "Now . . . where have I heard that before? Well, listen up, Kyle, the best way you can help me right now is to go away."

Kyle shook his head. "I can't do that, sir."

"Then get the hell out of my way while I go dress."

When Albert returned to the front hallway he was decked out in his salesman's costume. Starched white shirt. Red bow tie and suspenders. Gray tweed sports coat. Checkered brown trousers. White socks. A shiny pair of penny loafers.

Kyle was standing beside the front door. "Nice outfit," he grinned.

"Thanks. You have to *be* what your customers expect. Puts them at ease." Albert lifted his rain poncho from its peg. "You think it's going to rain today, Kyle?" he asked.

"I don't know, sir."

"Well, I don't think it will." He hung the poncho back up.

"I can't let you go out there, sir," Kyle said. "I'm here to protect you."

"You already said that. I'll tell you what . . . let's just crack open the door and see what the weather looks like. Okay? Open'er up, Kyle. It's okay."

Kyle pulled the door open.

"See," beamed Albert. "The sun's shining. Not a cloud in the sky. Used to call this 'Indian Summer' back in Chicago where I grew up."

Kyle said nothing as they stepped together out onto the porch.

"I'm going to work now, Kyle. The front door will lock when you close it."

"Jesus, Professor, you don't leave me with a lot of choices here."

"Bullshit! You've got all the choices in the world, Kyle. You can shoot me in the back if that's what you think you need to do. But remember this. Professor Chester Orinthal Brighton is already dead. He has been for a long, long time. Do you think that killing an insignificant used car dealer named Albert Benson is going to solve anything?"

Kyle did not respond.

"And another thing. Don't come around here again. Brighton won't be here. Ever again. Only Albert Benson." Suddenly he grinned.

"Unless, of course, you're looking for a good deal on a fine reconditioned single-owner used car. Then we might be able to do a little business. Now stand aside. I'm late for work."

Albert brushed past him and hustled down the sidewalk to the curb where a gleaming red Subaru bearing dealer's plates was parked. He yanked at the door and it creaked open. Then he straightened and called up to Kyle, "Tell Penny I still love her. And that I miss her."

Kyle nodded. "I will."

Albert thought for a moment, then added, "And tell her I'm sorry."

He ducked inside and the engine ground and sputtered and roared to life with a little explosion of white smoke from the exhaust pipe. Albert Benson waved to Kyle a final time and drove off into the splendid morning where all was well and the customers would be in a fine mood and primed to buy themselves each a spiffy new pre-owned automobile.

Ventriloquist

The Spring sunlight was warm. I must have dozed as I waited for Gloria on a bench in the downtown plaza. My eyes opened onto the eight-foot-tall bronze statue of William McKinley, planted on its concrete pedestal overlooking the still-living. *Something is inherently* odd *about it*, I decided, tipping my head back. *Misshapen*, it seemed. For one thing, the head was too large. And the gleaming statesman's coat, tarnished to a dull brown by the weather and wrapped about him like a burrito, was too cylindrical and barrel-like. The legs were stick-like and short. Maybe it was just my perspective from down below. Funny, though, that in all these years I never noticed how odd it was before.

Or maybe it was just the shock of my abrupt awakening. It had been an old memory, itself odd, that had done it. A recollection I had not even known was there. I had been daydreaming, looking out across the thick green weedy grass behind my grandmother's house in Missouri to where a scarecrow was planted at the edge of the corn. It made me uneasy at first. A deathlike black jacket had been buttoned around the wooden cross of a frame. The cloth rippled in the light, humid breeze. But an old straw hat was perched rakishly on its head, and that made me smile. Yes, I was a child, but I knew it was just a scarecrow. And I also knew that it was *alive*. It was as alive as those fellows I saw swinging their scythes in the distant courtyard behind the church. And I knew with an unreasonable clarity that it was *I* who quickened them all. Simply by observing them.

I wondered why that scarecrow was watching the chicken coop, which leaned behind the small, sun-blanched shed out back. What was he waiting for? What did he expect to see? I gazed over at the coop, but saw nothing but chickens. What was the scarecrow waiting for? A fox? And what would he do if one suddenly appeared. Nothing. I knew the scarecrow could do nothing. How frustrating it must be! But he was waiting nonetheless, if for no other reason than to watch. But what was Mr. Scarecrow *thinking* as he passed the time, waiting fecklessly? Now *that* was something that interested me. I was unable to imagine what it might be. If asked, what would he say? As I waited for him to speak, that dirty straw hat slowly turned, and he stared at me with an empty eyeless grin.

I shuddered awake, my eyes still gazing on the ghost of that sentient scarecrow. Then my lids opened lazily into the dazzling sunlight. They refocused on the unlikely likeness of President McKinley, who, I had recently read, was assassinated by a second-generation Polish socialist. Two pistol bullets had been fired point blank into the depths of his abdomen. His right hand was outstretched in what I had always thought to be an oratorical gesture of magnanimity, but which I now saw was with the intention of gripping the hand of the narrow-shouldered, blond-haired young stranger before him.

McKinley was in the first year of his second term, still smelling of victory. Victory in the Spanish-American war. Victory for him and his Rough Rider running mate over that arch rival, bible-thumping William Jennings Bryant. Victory for the second time in four years. Victory that had cleansed the path for him to pursue his new ambition of engaging the whole world in his mercantile vision.

What were those blank bronze eyes seeing? They took in the majestic Temple of Music at the Pan-American Exposition. Before him was the well-dressed, blond young anarchist with a handkerchief draped curiously over his right hand. McKinley raised his own to couple with that of the assassin, while the crowd assailed him with congratulations and orchestral music echoed and churned throughout the hall. Of this strange young man before him, this foreigner with all the zees in his last name who was calling himself "No Man" in German, the President knew nothing. Nothing, except that something was *odd* about the way the white handkerchief covered the right hand that rose to shake his own. What was the President about to say to him?

I glanced down at my wristwatch and grunted. Gloria was late. Her meeting had gone over by twenty minutes already. Oh well.

My eyes found the dead President's blank face again and pondered. Now, after two World Wars and Prohibition and the Roaring Twenties and the advent of nuclear warfare, after all the flower children had lowered their eyes to their hand-held devices, after the entire twentieth century had evaporated like an icicle . . . what was he seeing? What was he seeing *now*, more than a century after his death? What thoughts filled that bronze dome of a head? What would he *say to me now* if I asked?

My eyes caught Gloria entering the plaza from the opposite corner. In her crisp, dark-blue pantsuit, head down, she clacked purposefully toward me. Her black eyes flashed up at me, and I waved, but she dropped her gaze back to the sidewalk. She looked angry. Why was she angry? Was she angry with *me*? What had I done *this time* to make her angry with me? With Gloria it was always stormy. Inside that pretty head storm winds always blew. A tempest I could not see or feel directly, but one I knew was there. I sat up from my slouch and braced myself. What was she thinking *now*? What was she going to *say*?

And then, as she stood facing me in that severe blue suit, she smiled. "Hi," she said.

I stood and kissed her on the mouth.

In Which Universe?

*"Quantum mechanics insists on multiple simultaneous realities . . .
the 'real' reality to be determined by someone's measuring it."*
–Chopra and Leibstien, *General Unification Theory*

1

The vessels totaled four, three spaceships and the Anchor Pod. The spaceships didn't look like spaceships at all. At least not the kind in comic books and newsreels and movies I'd grown up with. No, each of the four vessels looked more like the rippling surface of a tightly swirling cloud and brought to mind sunlight sparkling on water. They had not been "built" in the classic sense. No, they had been "grown" almost instantaneously by clusters of lasers from accelerated quantumly-entangled high-energy particles. Now they tightly orbited the Lagrangian point L2, a half-million miles beyond the orbit of the moon.

You see, in order to attain the relativistic velocities necessary to fly to even the nearest stars and return home within a human life span, the physicists and engineers had needed to harness the power of quantum entanglement. In layman's terms, each vessel had been created from nothing. The Anchor Pod completed an irregular quantum tetrahedron, and was designed to remain gravitationally tethered at L2, lest the entire shooting match slip away and disappear with a flash into the boundless universe.

My name is Reuben Guilfoyle, Captain of the assigned tender *Antares* for the duration of the flight. Now "flight" can be a misleading moniker if it brings to mind the soaring of birds or airplanes, or the powered arc of traditional rockets. For the three quantum spaceships were not intended to "go" anywhere in the ordinary sense. Like the Anchor Pod, the ships' corporal presence was designed to remain in tight orbit around L2. Even the Chopra-Leibstien General Unification Theory does not permit anything to travel faster than the speed of light. But it does open the doorway to back-traveling a beam of light which has already made the journey here from the stars. The trick is to harness quantum entanglement of antithetical masses. No actual mass would be going anywhere, but quantum information could nonetheless be accessed and retrieved from far, far away. Or so the Theory predicts.

And that's what this entire experiment was about. Machines alone could not do the job, because of the weak anthropic principle. Humans had to participate, and human awareness, properly harnessed and focused, would make the quantum "journey." And I for one was curious as hell about what that experience might feel like.

This was all a tricky business. The entanglement process created each of the vessels around a "seed" that was one of four space-suited astronauts as they floated in empty space. Each vessel was quantum-linked to all the others. Two of the four vessels were composed of anti-matter, flavored real and imaginary. The other two were composed of ordinary matter, real and imaginary. The astronauts were supposed to be insulated from the vessel in which they dwelt by a continuously generated Chopra-Leibstien Field. Of course, the uncertainty principle would not entirely rule out the possibility of quantum contamination, although no one could imagine what that might look like. The astronauts, however, were cautioned and signed releases.

But the devilment gets trickier. The problem was, no one knew which was which, matter or anti-matter, real or imaginary, and that critical information could never be measured without breaking the essential quantum entanglement. This difficulty would be of no importance in the outbound journey, since the three spacecraft would be projected in oblique trajectories, each roughly perpendicular to the others. But it certainly would matter on their return. These four starfaring vessels could never be allowed to bump into each other, for such an encounter of matter and anti-matter would annihilate both with an instantaneous release of energy defined by Einstein's famous equation.

I knew two of the astronauts well. Better than well. I had dated Ulrike years ago when we were all testing aircraft at Edwards. She was the most beautiful woman I had ever met. And the most competent. It was I who introduced her to Hank Ostrander in what was probably the worst move of my life. She found Hank's devil-may-care professional-ism irresistible. They were married four months later, just before she left to finish her doctorate in astrophysics at Berkeley. But we all remained close friends over the years as our careers led us down different, but converging paths.

2

"This is Pod Com," said Ulrike Ostrander, the Commander in the Anchor Pod. "Can everyone read me?"

"Ship One," replied Ho Gen Ming, the Chinese astronaut, "reading you loud and clear."

"Ship Two," reported Ivan Denisovich Kraken, his Russian counterpart. "You I read too."

Silence.

"Hank, are you there?"

"Yeah, sorry, hon," came Hank Ostrander's voice from the third spaceship. "Ship Three here. I can read you loud and clear."

"All right. Looks like we're good to go," Ulrike radioed. Only of course it really wasn't a radio transmission at all, since they all occupied the same quantum space and time together, however distant the vessels might move apart. The "transmission" was more akin to a quiet conversation. Pillow talk, as Hank called it. But outdated concepts die hard sometimes. "On my mark we will begin continual communication through the completion of the mission," she said. "I will maintain contact and relay everything directly to AtaCom, so watch what you say. It's all going into the history books."

"Roger," replied Hank.

"Understood," acknowledged Ivan.

"As was it all explained," said Ho.

"Okay . . . ready . . . *mark*."

"Let's get on our way," urged her husband.

"AtaCom, this is Anchor Pod." Ulrike spoke into her shoulder mike, for this was a real radio transmission. "We're ready to go."

After a four-second delay came, "Anchor Pod, Atacama. Every-thing looks good from down here. You are clear to launch at will. Good luck and godspeed."

Of course there could be no external control of the quantum vessels as in launches of old. Time would run at a different rate on earth and in the vessels once they were underway. For them the whole voyage, if all went well, would take eight to twelve hours. One long day of work. Estimates of how much time would pass on earth varied from a few weeks to many months. Indeed, measuring and comparing lapsed time was to be a major objective of the mission.

"Roger, AtaCom." From her position inside the Anchor Pod there was no control panel to be seen. No windshield. No seat. No ship. To her senses she was floating weightlessly in space in her spacesuit with her helmet and gloves off and tethered beside her. The air she breathed shouldn't have been there, but it was. Just like a day at the beach. "You guys ready?"

"Ship One, ready."

"Ship Two, good to go."

"Ship Three, what're we waiting for?"

Ulrike gazed down at the control bracelet wreathing her left wrist. Her pulse was racing over 130 bpm. She drew a deep breath. "Okay. Here goes." She touched the countdown button, ". . . four, three, two, one, *launch*."

3

They all felt a sense of acceleration. Even Ulrike thought she felt it, though it may have been a contact high. The minds of the other three were accelerating up beams of light at almost instantaneous velocity. Ho toward Alpha Centauri. Ivan toward the binary stars of Procyn. And Hank on his way to Ross 128.

"*PodCom! Do you read?*"

"Yes, Ivan, I'm right here. No need to shout."

"I too close to target. Things weird here. Hot. You draw me back, no?"

"How far?"

"Do not know. Try point zero zero two."

Ulrike punched the numbers into a slider on her bracelet. "How's that?"

"Too far. Go back point zero zero one."

"Roger. How's that? What are you seeing?"

"Is incredible!" He fell silent.

"Anybody else need a tweak? Ho, how're you doing?"

"It is so beautiful," came Ho's soft voice, as if he were sitting next to her. "I looking around. Take photos."

"Hank? Are you there?"

"I'm here, hon. I wish you could see this. Everything is so red. Like being inside a ruby. I think I see the planet. It's ocean looks . . . purplish. If you're not too busy, I'd like to see if you can set me down on it."

"I'm not sure we can do that. Let me get everyone else settled first. Then we can give it a try."

4

My ship was based in Lunar orbit. Every 29.5 days the *Antares* would make its rounds of the four quantum vessels. My job was to visually inspect them and the nuclear generators whose beams powered the quantum tetrahedron. I had signed on to a one-year commission, but my service was to be extended much longer than anyone had expected.

The data stream from the Anchor Pod came in at ever-decreasing frequencies, as was expected. Many days of data had to be saved and compressed to reconstruct even a single short transmission. The people in mission control, and, indeed, all over the whole world, hung on every word and photo and bit of telemetry. Incredibly, everything seemed to be working as designed. But with time the data slowed. More and more. After almost a year, a day finally came when the data stopped entirely. Virtual velocity had reached a steady state at the speed of light. Either that or a catastrophic failure had occurred. No one knew which. Thirteen months had passed since the day of launch. It was taking a lot longer than planned. As the weeks dragged by, the public began to lose interest.

Then, two months after the loss of signal, a single bit of data arrived. A day later, another. Then two. Then three. The scientists cheered. The astronauts had turned around. They were on their way back home. The speed of the data increased. Soon the scientists were going wild as it began to pour in in torrents. Visuals from the helmet and shoulder cameras. Readouts from the instruments. But most fascinating seemed to be the verbal descriptions by the astronauts themselves. Descriptions of things no human had ever before experienced.

5

"AtaCom, PodCom here. My instruments show we're back."

Four second pause. "We're showing the same thing down here. Congratulations and welcome home. Two of the generators have been showing signs of strain, so we want to go ahead and run the shut-down checklist as soon as we can."

We followed each step in the check-list. The astronauts fastened on their helmets and gloves and verified the seals and that the cooling and oxygen systems were functioning properly. Then it was my job to synchronize the shutdown of the generators. The decoherence process had to be precise so that the matter and antimatter vessels would evaporate at precisely the same instant. Nothing returning to nothing without a bump or a hitch or even a hiccup was the goal. It was a slow, balanced procedure, but after about fifty minutes the vessels all winked out of existence together, leaving the astronauts floating again in empty space.

Well, *almost* empty space.

"PodCom, Ship Two. I have sparking."

"Sparking? Describe the situation, Ivan."

"Sparking on spacesuit–*Ow! ow!–that was big one–suit breached–*" The transmission fell silent.

"Ivan?"

No response.

"Ship Two, do you read?"

Ivan did not transmit again. The unthinkable had happened. Each astronaut had taken on the matter state of his or her vessel. Thus two astronauts, like their vessels, were constituted of ordinary matter. But two were composed of anti-matter. Ivan's suit had interacted with particles of ordinary matter in the far reaches of earth's upper atmosphere.

Something as simple as a hydrogen atom was enough to create a "spark" as it annihilated itself with a particle of the space suit.

"Ulrike, this is Hank. Anyone else sparking?"

No response.

"There's one more of us out here. In the same state as Ivan. Who is it?"

Silence.

"Ulrike? Is it you?"

"I've had a couple of sparks, Hank. It might be something else."

"*Dear God, no! Please! Not you Ulrike.* I'm coming for you. *Antares* do you read?"

"I'm here Hank."

"Is that you Reuben?"

"It's me."

"Come pick me up."

"No can do. I've gotta–"

"*Now! Pick me up!*"

"Ho's next up on my orders–"

"He'll be alright. Right, Ho?"

"I be okay," came Ho's voice. "Oxygen 93 percent. No sparking."

"*Dammit Reuben, pick me up. Ferry me to Ulrike!*"

I broke my orders. Brought the *Antares* about and headed for Hank. Maybe not so much for his sake, as for Ulrike's. When AtaCom came on I tuned them out with "Something's wrong with my radio."

I saw him as a bright speck in the sunlight and reversed the thrusters as I drew alongside. The sun cast a lopsided halo around the earth. We were beyond its umbra. I donned my helmet and gloves and cycled open the airlock. Hank was floating about ten meters off port.

"You coming aboard?" I asked.

"Pong me first," he said. "Can't be too careful. Have to be sure."

I detached the air gun from my belt and inserted one of those little hollow plastic balls. "Ready?" I asked.

"Ready," he replied.

I fired the ball at him and would have missed if he hadn't used his suit thrusters to intercept it. The ball caromed harmlessly off his chest in the direction of the crescent moon. "It's not me," he said. "And I don't think it's Ho. You've got to take me to Ulrike."

"You might be going to your own funeral," I said.

"Maybe. Maybe not. Nothing is certain in quantum mechanics."

He wouldn't come inside the ship, but clung to the grab irons around the door. I think he was afraid I wouldn't let him out again. I turned the ship toward Ulrike. "PodCom, we're on our way."

"Don't do this, Reuben. It's suicide. I'm sparking. There's nothing either of you can do."

"We made a pact, Ulrike," Hank broke in. "We talked about this happening, and we made a pact."

"That was before. This is now. I free you from that pact."

"Not that easy."

"Hank, be reasonable. You've got a whole life ahead of your. You're a hero now. You'll find someone else."

"But I don't want someone else. She wouldn't be you."

I listened in to their radio transmission as I piloted the spacecraft toward a gleaming speck hovering in the starry sky. It was not like eavesdropping. I was a part of this. I loved her too. Always had. Always will.

"I see her, Reuben," Hank said. "Set a direct course."

I checked the instruments. "Dead on course," I told him.

"Okay, I'm letting go," he said. "Pull up and get the hell out of here. Just in case."

I imagine that before long Hank could make out her features. He began retarding with his suit thrusters. Occasionally a spark would flash brightly against her suit. "Do you still have pressure?" he asked.

"I've got the tank wide open and it's holding well enough. For now. You big dumb lug."

I can picture him grinning at her. Loving every line of her gentle face through the two panes of glass as they drifted closer.

"It's not too late to turn back," she said.

"Yes it is," he said. "Far too late. Now you just give me one of those big bear hugs of yours, sweetie."

White light blazed for an instant, as brilliant as a newborn quasar. It pierced the fabric of space-time, bending it into multiple simultaneous realities and other dimensions, and was swallowed. Darkness closed in again.

6

    "Hank?"

    "Hmm?"

    "Are you awake?"

    "Um."

    "Open your eyes."

    Hank drew a deep breath. The air was sharp and ripe and tangy. Ruby light filtered through strange contrasting foliage, like a Henri Rousseau painting viewed under lurid red light. The ground was covered with soft blocks, like reptile scales, vibrating gently. *I know this place,* he thought vaguely.

    "Hank?"

    Their spacesuits were gone. He held her tighter in his arms. "Yeah, hon?"

    "Where are we?"

Vanishing Point

Two billion people walked this earth the day my grandfather was born. "Each one," he said to me, "from his or her own isolated well of consciousness, claims to be the center of the universe." By 2030 the population had exploded to over eight billion. I remember my grandfather complaining, "My own significance shrinks to the vanishing point."

Now I count myself among the few who are left. Maybe three-hundred-million of us, give or take. No one is really counting any more. My own personal worth soars as the species plummets toward extinction. Like the stock market. Supply and demand. We have saved the planet, but lost the human race.

The decisive moment came when the United Nations adopted its solution to the problem of human overpopulation. Bangladesh and other coastal nations were losing ground to rising seas. India and China were swamped with human flesh and hungry mouths. There were not enough resources to go around. Stresses fractured along religious and racial fault lines. Civil conflicts erupted into regional wars. Refugees fled the horror, but neighboring countries closed their borders, defending them with razor wire and lethal force. Political order was teetering worldwide. Something had to be done to prevent a descent into barbarism.

So the Security Council ordered XOL22 to be introduced into the atmosphere all over the world by high-soaring aircraft. XOL22 was a simple contraceptive aerosol designed to prevent human conception. The aerosol had been contrived by an international consortium of scientists as a living organism able to evolve its own defenses. To defeat cheaters.

There was an antidote. FERTILE7 was made available only to those women with government-issued licenses to conceive and give birth. Meeting reasonable, but not particularly onerous standards of health, education, and financial ability to raise and nurture offspring was all that was required. Quotas were set for each country. The standards and quotas were established by an impartial commission from measurements and calculations of the earth's capacity to sustain a population.

In the short term, the systems performed remarkably well (although religious zealots and personal-rights fanatics would never agree). Almost immediately the world's total population began a downward arc toward the desired asymptote of five billion inhabitants. But the Security Council edict, admittedly even-handed and well-intended, has lead to an even more grievous consequence than overpopulation.

As everyone knows, the antidote FERTILE7 began to lose its effectiveness almost immediately. That was years ago. The atmosphere and waters of the entire planet were contaminated with XOL22. In the warming atmosphere the aerosol evolved its defenses. It bound to the hydrogen-oxygen bonds and could not be removed, even by distillation. The brightest minds could not find a substitute for FERTILE7. New births dwindled, then stopped altogether.

No one has been born for more than ninety years now, and the population has aged without replacement. Our numbers have now shrunk to a pitiable few old folks. And even fewer of us will see another decade pass. As a consequence, the increasingly pressing problem has now become: how do we preserve all human knowledge and history and culture beyond the end of mankind? In my opinion, the Meme Bank Project, for all its faults, holds the greatest promise.

We are now old, feeble, demented. We can no longer do the work required with our own minds and hands. The task is beyond our abilities. So we have programmed machines to collect and organize and catagorize the data and implement the project. We call them the Curators. Artificial intelligence. Self-replicating. Self-improving. Evolving. We have no way of knowing what they will become. Who can say? Maybe by cataloging and storing and comparing and studying us and our wit, a little will rub off. Perhaps the Curators will become witty themselves. And perhaps even compassionate. Maybe they will even become "human." God knows we have bequeathed them everything we know. There is nothing more we can do. I often wonder what a cosmonaut from a distant star might find should he ever happen upon this insignificant planet in the remote future.

As for myself, I remain philosophical. Stoic even. Perhaps a bit solipsistic. For me the world will end when I die, whether or not there is anyone left to carry the banner of humanity. There will be no one left to mourn the loss. Or to read this memorandum. It is impossible to ignore the irony of what we have done to ourselves. The religious fanatics proved to be right after all, and at times I cannot but smile at God's final joke on us.

This will be my last memo. The situation is now out of my hands. I have made my recommendation to the President, as have others. I have argued in favor of the Meme Bank, of course. Whatever other consequences it might portend, it seems to hold the greatest promise of preserving human culture beyond the final collapse. Beyond that, there is really not much I can say. I am going to send this memo now and shut down my computer. Then I am going home to tend the flowers and wait for the sun to set.

About the Author

Richard S. Platz maintained a solo law practice in Humboldt County, California, for 35 years. He served as City Attorney for the City of Blue Lake for 32 of those years before retiring there in 2009. In addition to these short stories, the author has written two other books of short stories entitled *Memories and other Fictions* and *Dreamtime*. He has also written the novels *Appointment At Angahuan* (with James A. Kline), *Of Magic and Delusion*, and *Project Divine Wind*. Additional short stories, poetry, and articles on various topics, including the popular *Backpacking in Jefferson*, can be read on his website: www.richardplatz.com.

www.ingramcontent.com/pod-product-compliance
Lightning Source LLC
Chambersburg PA
CBHW060044150626
46556CB00018BA/2693